CLASSIFIED

CODE NAME
BANANAS

David Walliams

CLASSIFIED

CODE NAME
BANANAS

Illustrated by Tony Ross

HarperCollins *Children's Books*

Thank you to Julie and her family for naming the gorilla "Gertrude".
Julie won the competition I created with Comic Relief and
BBC Children in Need to name a character in this book.
Thank you to all of you who entered the competition.

David Walliams

First published in hardback in Great Britain by
HarperCollins *Children's Books* in 2020
Published in this paperback edition 2022
HarperCollins *Children's Books* is a division of HarperCollins*Publishers* Ltd,
1 London Bridge Street
London SE1 9GF

www.harpercollins.co.uk

HarperCollins*Publishers*
1st Floor, Watermarque Building, Ringsend Road
Dublin 4, Ireland

1

Text copyright © David Walliams 2020
Illustrations copyright © Tony Ross 2020
Cover lettering of author's name copyright © Quentin Blake 2010
All rights reserved.

ISBN 978–0–00–847180–4

David Walliams and Tony Ross assert the moral right to be
identifi ed as the author and illustrator of the work respectively.

For James & Sophie,

With love,

David x

CLASSIFIED

THANK-YOUS

I WOULD LIKE TO THANK:

ANN-JANINE MURTAGH
My Executive Publisher

CHARLIE REDMAYNE
CEO

TONY ROSS
My Illustrator

PAUL STEVENS
My Literary Agent

HARRIET WILSON
My Editor

KATE BURNS
Art Editor

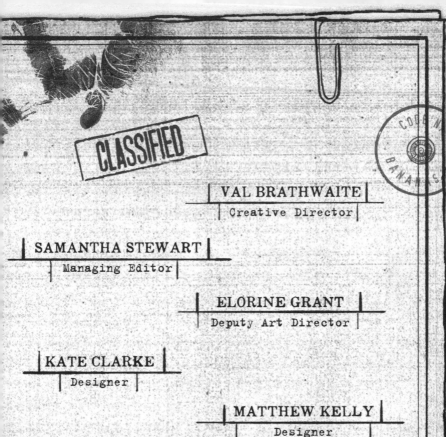

CLASSIFIED

VAL BRATHWAITE
| Creative Director |

SAMANTHA STEWART
| Managing Editor |

ELORINE GRANT
| Deputy Art Director |

KATE CLARKE
| Designer |

MATTHEW KELLY
| Designer |

SALLY GRIFFIN
| Designer |

GERALDINE STROUD
| My PR Director |

TANYA HOUGHAM
| Audio Producer |

David Walliams

LONDON

December 1940 | Second World War

CLASSIFIED

Britain has been in a bitter war
with Nazi Germany for over a year.
It is the height of the Blitz, and
Nazi bombs rain down on the city.
The people of London live in fear.
As do the animals of the city,
particularly those in LONDON ZOO.

The characters in our adventure are...

ERIC

This short, shy eleven-year-old boy has
sticky-out ears and wears glasses with one
of the lenses cracked. Sadly, like many
children of the time, Eric has lost both his
parents in the war. Now an orphan, he is
withdrawn and sad most of the time. The only
thing that makes the boy happy is visiting
LONDON ZOO. There he has formed a very
special friendship with a huge furry friend.
More of her, in a moment.

UNCLE SID

Sid is Eric's great-uncle, and the oldest keeper at **LONDON ZOO**. He has worked there for longer than anyone can remember, including him. Like many men at the outbreak of the First World War, he enlisted to become a soldier. However, on his very first day on the battlefields of France, he stepped on an enemy mine, and lost both his legs. Nowadays Sid gets about on tin legs, but nothing can dampen his fighting spirit. The zookeeper would give anything to be able to battle the Nazis and prove himself to be a hero once and for all.

GRANDMA

Eric's grandmother is a fearsome character. She
dresses from head to toe in black: black shoes,
black coat and black pillbox hat. The deaf old
lady never goes anywhere without her ear trumpet,
which helps her hear. This doubles as a weapon to
bash folks out of her way. When Eric became an
orphan, she took the boy in to live with her. As
much as he loves his grandmother, Eric finds it
hard to be around her as she is so very strict.

BESSIE

Bessie is a larger-than-life
lady, bursting with love and
laughter. She works as a doctor
in a military hospital in
London, where day and night she
tends to the wounded soldiers.
Bessie and Sid are next-door
neighbours, living side by side
in a row of tiny terraced houses.
A bomb blast tore a hole in the
fence that divides their back
gardens, so Bessie can pop round
to see Sid at any time of the day
or night.

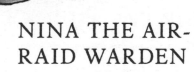

NINA THE AIR-RAID WARDEN

Nina is one of London's hundreds
of air-raid wardens, who spring
into action when the Nazi bombers
appear. Wardens make sure that
Londoners are off the streets and
taking shelter whenever the air-
raid warning sounds. It is the
perfect job for this busybody,
who loves nothing more than
bossing folk around.

SIR FREDERICK FROWN

Considering Frown is the Director General of
LONDON ZOO, it may come as a surprise to
you that he doesn't like animals. Creatures
of all shapes and sizes give him the willies.
Frown is forever in fear of being slobbered
over, nibbled or, worst of all, peed on. So
he spends most of the time hiding in his office,
as far away from all those dreadful beasts as
possible. He is so achingly posh he speaks
as if he has a plum in his mouth.

CORPORAL BATTER

This old soldier from the First World War is now the nightwatchman at **LONDON ZOO**. Batter sports a big, bushy moustache and is never without his tin helmet, his chest full of medals and, most importantly, his rifle. Batter has strict orders to shoot any dangerous animals that escape from the zoo during the night-time bombing raids.

MISS GNARL

This tall, broad vet at **LONDON ZOO** is called whenever an animal needs to be put down. Armed with a needle full of poison, the sinister Gnarl adores her work. The bigger the animal, the better. She is a disturbing character, who speaks only in growls.

HELENE and BERTHA

These mysterious elderly twin sisters run a deserted guesthouse at the British seaside town of Bognor Regis. The guesthouse, Seaview Towers, has not had a guest for years. So, what are the strange pair doing there? Perhaps their glamorous appearance hides something darker below the surface.

CAPTAIN SPEER

Speer is the elegant but ruthless commander
of a Nazi U-boat (or submarine). The Führer
Adolf Hitler himself, the evil Nazi leader
who seized power in Germany, has personally
sent Speer on a top-secret mission. This
mission has taken the U-boat to the south
coast of Britain, where it is lurking, ready
to strike. If Speer succeeds, the course of
the war will take a dramatic turn, making a
Nazi victory certain.

WINSTON CHURCHILL

The British prime minister is a big,
balding man, always dressed immaculately
in three-piece suits, bowties and Homburg
hats. Winston Churchill is famous for his
stirring speeches, his dogged determination
and his fondness for brandy and cigars. He
is seen by many as the only leader who can
lead Britain to victory over the Nazis.

And last but not least...

GERTRUDE THE GORILLA

One of the oldest animals at **LONDON ZOO**,
Gertrude is also the most popular. She is the
zoo's star attraction. Children delight in
the old ape's escapades, as she loves to show
off for the crowds, especially for a banana
or two. Gertrude loves to blow raspberries at
the visitors. The gorilla has formed a special
friendship with one child in particular. A
short, shy boy in cracked glasses who goes by
the name of Eric.

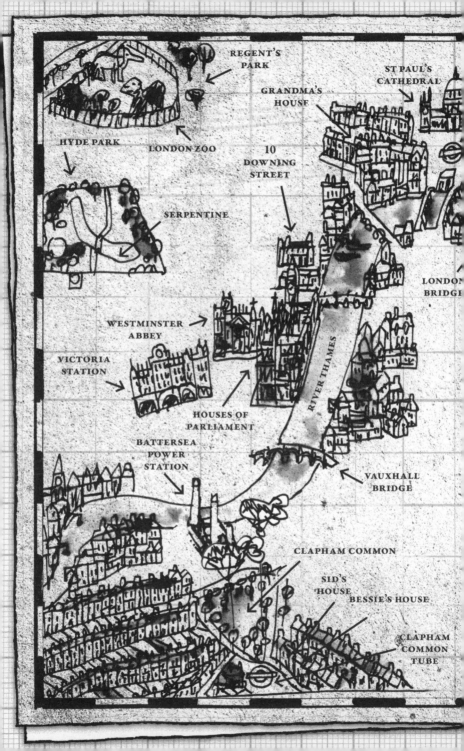

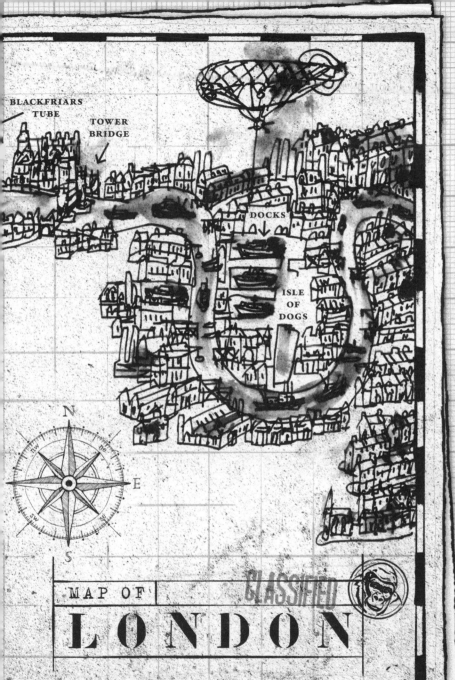

BLACKFRIARS
TUBE

TOWER
BRIDGE

DOCKS

ISLE
OF
DOGS

N

S

E

MAP OF

CLASSIFIED

LONDON

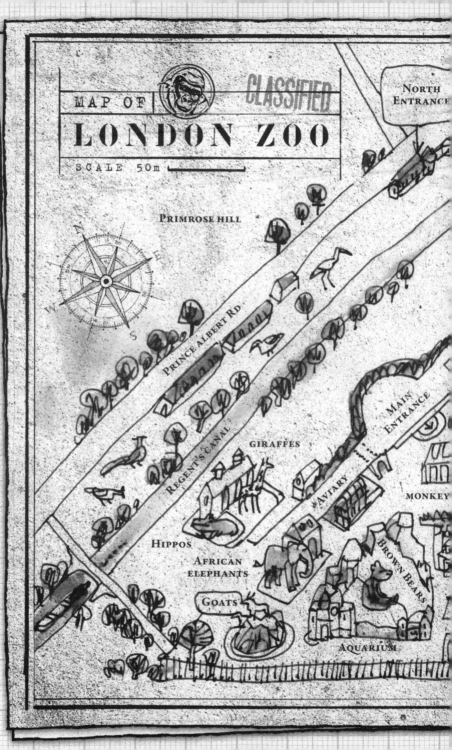

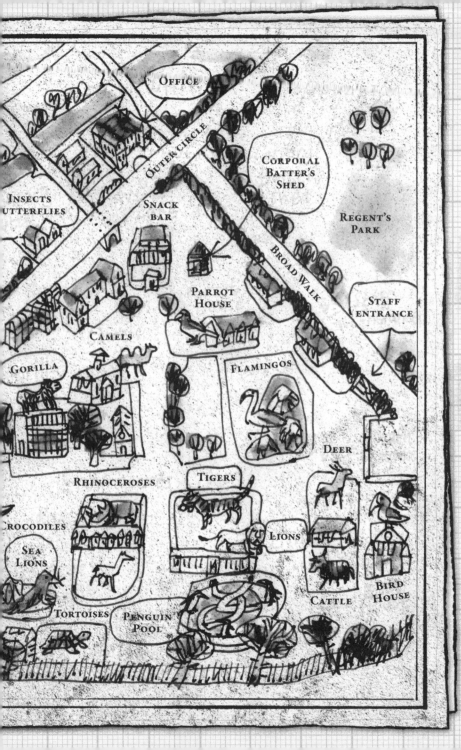

PART ONE

TIME TO DARE

CB

CLASSIFIED

WIBBLE WOBBLE

Life.
Love.
Laughter.

The world had been plunged into a war of unimaginable horror, so these three things were more important than ever.

They are important to this story too.

Our adventure begins on a cold, crisp afternoon in London in December 1940. In **LONDON ZOO,** to be precise. There, a little boy had just made a discovery. A discovery that made him laugh for the first time in a long, long time.

"HA! HA! HA!"

That little boy was an eleven-year-old orphan named Eric. He was

27

short for his age and had sticky-out ears, which made him feel like *he* stuck out. The boy wore glasses, but one of the lenses was cracked, and he didn't have any money to repair them.

As soon as the bell rang for the end of school, Eric would run out of the gates as fast as his little legs would take him. He hated school, where he

was picked on mercilessly for his sticky-out ears, and given the nickname "Wingnut".

Eric had been given strict orders by his grandmother to hurry straight home. But he couldn't resist taking a detour. From school, he dashed through the streets, dodging the mountains of rubble. There were adventures to be had in the wreckage of downed Nazi planes, burnt-out double-decker buses or bombed buildings, but the boy didn't dilly-dally. Oh no. He was in a rush to get to his favourite place on earth.

LONDON ZOO.

Apart from all the animals, the best thing about the zoo was that Eric could get in for FREE! That was because his uncle worked there as a zookeeper. Uncle Sid was really his mum's uncle, but Eric always called the old man "Uncle Sid" too. Sometimes Eric would even help Sid with his work. This he loved more than anything. His dream was to be a zookeeper himself one day. To Eric, animals seemed so much nicer than humans. None of them made fun of his sticky-out ears for a start. Some of them had sticky-out ears too. No matter, they were all beautiful in their own way.

Eric loved feeding the animals, washing them and he didn't even mind mucking out their cages. Some elephant droppings weighed a ton and shovelling them was a two-man job.

A Spotter's Guide to
ANIMAL DROPPINGS:

ANT   PIRANHA   SCORPION

PENGUIN   ARMADILLO   ZEBRA

TIGER   GORILLA   CAMEL

RHINOCEROS   ELEPHANT

Sid would smuggle Eric in through the back entrance to the zoo. That way he would not have to pay the entrance fee of sixpence, a small fortune for a small boy. Eric didn't have a penny to his name, let alone six.

So, at four o'clock on the dot each day, Eric would arrive at the staff gate. In what resembled a military operation, he would remain out of sight and knock three times.

KNOCK! KNOCK! KNOCK!

Then he would wait in silence until he heard a "Twit-twoo!" This was his great-uncle imitating the call of an owl. That sound meant the coast was clear. The next thing the boy would hear was the old man approaching. Sid had tin legs. His real ones had been blown off in the First World War. Whenever he walked, there was the sound of clinking, clanking and clunking.

CLINK! CLANK! CLUNK!

"Password!" the man would hiss, hiding on the other side of the gate.

"Wibble wobble!" the boy would reply.

"Ha! Ha!" chuckled Sid as he opened the gate. "In you come!"

The password was different every day. The boy

would invent a new one each time to make his great-uncle laugh.

Some of their favourites were:

MONKEY NUTS   KING PONG

ANTS IN YOUR PANTS

NICKY NACKY NOO

HIPPOPOTOMOUSTACHE

WEE WILLY WINKY   JELLY BOTTOM

FINKY FOO-FAR   UDDER FUDDER

SIR HUMPHREY HANDBAG

"Thanks, Uncle Sid."

"How was school today?" asked the old man. There was a strong family resemblance. Sid was short and had sticky-out ears too. However, he also had big, bushy eyebrows and an even bushier beard, so that was where the family resemblance ended. Because of his tin legs the old man was unsteady on his feet, which were also made of tin. Sid looked like he was going to topple over at any moment.

"I hate it!" huffed the boy.

"I don't know why I bother asking!"

"The kids pick on me about my ears."

"Your ears look perfectly normal to me!" said the old man as he waggled his own sticky-out ears with his hands to make the boy laugh.

"Ha! Ha!"

"Don't let the bullies get you down! It's what's in here that counts," said Sid, clutching his heart. "You are a **smashing** boy – don't ever forget that!"

"I will try not to."

"Don't you have any friends at school?"

"Not really," replied the boy sorrowfully.

"Well, I know all the animals here are your friends. They love you as much as you love them."

The boy hugged the old man, nestling his head in Sid's big, round tummy.

"Whoa!" exclaimed Sid, flapping his arms around as if he were a penguin trying to take off.

"Sorry! I always forget about those tin legs…"

"Don't worry. You'll be able to sell me off for scrap metal when I'm gone!" he joked.

The boy smiled. "You're funny!"

"There may be a war on, but you have to keep smiling. And laughing. Or what else are we fighting for?"

"I had never thought of it like that," pondered the boy. "But you are right, Uncle Sid. Do you need a hand with anything today?"

"Oh! You are a good boy, but I've done all the mucking out. You go and enjoy yourself!"

"Thanks! I always do!"

"I know the animals will be pleased to see you after last night!"

The boy immediately knew what he meant. Last night had been the worst bombing raid by the Nazi air force (or "Luftwaffe") in London since the war had begun.

"As soon as the air-raid warning went off, I woke Granny up. She doesn't hear too good."

"Yes, I know! She's deaf as a post."

"And even though I was still in my pyjamas and Granny was in her nightdress we ran to **BLACKFRIARS TUBE**. We slept the night down in the station with hundreds of others, right there on the platform."

"How was it?" asked the old man. "Noisy, I bet."

"And smelly. Not the best night's sleep I've ever had!"

"No, but at least you and Granny were safe."

"Where did you hide out?"

"Me? The air-raid warden ordered me to run for shelter, but I came straight here to the zoo. I had to be here to take care of the animals. Try to keep them calm."

The boy winced at the thought of them all suffering. "How were they?"

"I did my best, but the bombs just kept on coming. **Boom! Boom! Boom!** I'm afraid to say your friend took it hardest. She can't bear the noise of the bombs. Frightened out of her wits, she was."

The boy gulped with fear. "I'd better go and see her right away."

"You do that. I know you always cheer her up like no one else can!"

The old man ruffled the boy's hair. Eric ran off in search of his friend.

To Eric, **LONDON ZOO** was a wonderland. He had never been outside London in his life, but here in just a few acres of the city were the most magical creatures from all over the world.

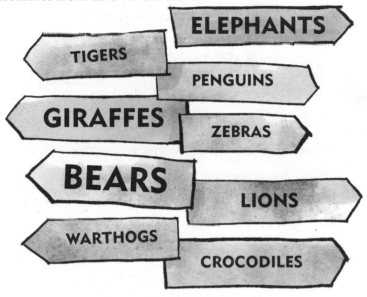

But there was one animal in particular that Eric loved more than any other.

Her name was Gertrude.
Gertrude the gorilla.

CHAPTER 2

MUDDLE

The funny thing about Gertrude was that she was so human, and so not human all at once.

Thick black hair covered her entire body, like a giant fur coat. Her head was enormous, with a bulging forehead as long as her face. Two unusually large ears stuck out on the sides of the gorilla's head, just above her eyes. Gorillas normally have tiny ears, but not Gertrude. Perhaps that is why the boy felt a special connection to her. Or perhaps it was her warm ginger eyes that flashed with kindness.

The gorilla's wide nose was wrinkled like an old lady's. This was fitting, as Gertrude was an old lady. She was fifty, positively ancient for a gorilla. But the thought that she was some sweet old dear would be gone the moment she opened her mouth.

FANGS!

Gertrude had the most magnificent set of fangs, two up and two down.

Also not sweet-old-dear-y were her arms. They were nearly as broad as her legs, and her legs were already broader than broad. What's more, her huge tummy was round like a barrel. The things Eric loved most about his best friend were her hands and feet. They were much like his, except they were absolutely

HUMONGOUS.

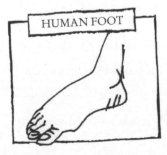

HUMAN FOOT

GORILLA FOOT

Gertrude might have been the biggest of all the apes in **LONDON ZOO**, but she was also the gentlest. Sometimes a sparrow would fly into her cage and land on her head. You might think that a gorilla, with its incredible strength, would crush an uninvited visitor in its hand. But not Gertrude. No, she would treat the little bird like a baby. The gorilla would hold it delicately in her hand and stroke it. Sometimes she would even mimic the birdsong.

"TWEET! TWEET!"

Then she would give the little creature a kiss on the beak.

"MWAH!"

All this would delight the crowds who would gather around Gertrude's cage. The gorilla was **LONDON ZOO'S STAR ATTRACTION.**

The worst thing about being an orphan was missing being hugged. Eric had lost his mum and dad during the war. They were both good at hugs. Sometimes they would even have a big family cuddle, with Eric in

the middle. They called
it a **MUDDLE.** Cuddle and
middle.

The boy loved those
muddles most of all.
Feeling the love and warmth
of both his parents made him
feel safe. Now the war had
torn them away from him.

Forever.

Eric knew he would
never have that feeling
again. So, when he gazed through the bars of Gertrude's
cage, he often wished he could magic his way inside.
Then the gorilla could just wrap her big strong arms
round him and hold him tight. Gertrude was as big as
both his parents put together. Eric was sure she could
give him a jolly good **muddle.**

CHAPTER | 3 | CLASSIFIED

PARTY TRICKS

Eric had dashed past animal after animal until he finally reached his best friend's cage. To his sadness he saw Gertrude the gorilla squatting in the corner with her back to the crowd, rocking to and fro.

This was not right.

Something was **very wrong.**

The old girl was not her normal self at all. Usually she would delight in showing off to the crowd, getting up to all sorts of tricks, especially for a banana. **Or two. Or three.** Or as many as she could stuff in her gob at once. Which was a lot.

Gertrude's **favourite** party tricks included:

STICKING OUT HER TONGUE

WAGGLING HER BOTTOM

BEATING HER CHEST

SALUTING LIKE A SOLDIER

PUTTING HER FINGERS IN HER EARS

PEELING A BANANA WITH HER FEET

SWINGING ON HER ROPE LIKE TARZAN

FLATTENING HER NOSE RIGHT UP AGAINST THE BARS OF HER CAGE

PERFORMING A CARTWHEEL

GIVING THE CROWD
A ROYAL WAVE

BLOWING A BANANA UP INTO THE AIR WITH
HER MOUTH, AND CATCHING IT AGAIN

PRETENDING
TO SLIP ON A
BANANA SKIN

ROLLING AROUND IN
THE STRAW, HOOTING
WITH LAUGHTER

COPYING THE WALK OF ANYONE
PASSING BY, ESPECIALLY THAT OF
THE UPTIGHT ZOO DIRECTOR GENERAL
HIMSELF, SIR FREDERICK FROWN

The boy couldn't bear seeing his friend looking so sad today. Last night's bombing raid had clearly frightened the life out of her. The crowd gathered around her cage were muttering and moaning.

"I paid good money for this!"

"Fat lot of good that gorilla is!"

"What a waste of time!"

Eric couldn't get through all the people, so he climbed up on top of a bench and shouted, "GERTRUDE!"

The moment the gorilla heard her friend's voice, she stopped rocking and stood up. Then she leaped on to her rope and shimmied up with ease, using her hands and feet. Once at the top, she spotted the boy over the sea of heads.

"EEH-AAH!" she cried on seeing Eric. Despite it being ear-splittingly loud,

you could tell it was a

happy cry.

CHAPTER 4

BLOWING RASPBERRIES

All those in the crowd looked around to spot who exactly this gorilla was so excited to see. Eric was painfully shy. Such was his embarrassment at being stared at that he blushed redder than a tomato.

Eric gave a little wave back to his friend. Then the crowd parted to let the boy go to the front.

Gertrude shimmied down the rope with ease and lolloped over to Eric. He put his hand up against the metal bars.

"Be careful!" came a shout from the crowd.

"Gorillas are dangerous!" came another.

"It will rip your arm off quicker than you can say Jack Sprat!" warned a third.

The gorilla followed the boy's lead. Gently, she placed her hand up against the bars from the inside. Now the palms of their hands were just touching.

Eric smiled, and Gertrude smiled back. Seeing her big silly smile made him chuckle, and Gertrude hooted with laughter too.

"Ha! Ha!"

"HEE-HAW! HEE-HAW!"

Then the boy stuck his tongue out at her.

Then the gorilla stuck her tongue out at him!

There was a ripple of laughter through the crowd.

"HA! HA! HΛ!"

Hearing them, Eric felt flustered and took a step back.

"Go on, boy!" someone prompted.

"Don't stop now!" urged another.

"This is worth the price of admission alone!" remarked a third.

The boy took a deep breath and tried to put all these strangers out of his mind. Summoning all his courage, he stepped towards the cage again. Gertrude smiled at him, her eyes twinkling. Eric smiled back. The gorilla's smiles were infectious.

Today the boy was determined to try to go one further: to teach Gertrude a new trick. So Eric did something that always made him chuckle. He blew a raspberry.

"PFFT!"

There were tuts and murmurs of disapproval from some of the grown-ups.

"TUT!"

"TUT!"

"TUT!"

Clearly, they were unimpressed with his childish humour.

But the gorilla was not. Gertrude looked puzzled for a moment. Then she pursed her lips and blew, but no sound came out. Egging her on to try again, the boy slowly pursed his lips, pushed his tongue forward, and blew.

"PFFFFT!"

"TUT!"

"TUT!"

"TUT!"

Looking at Eric the entire time for encouragement, the gorilla copied him. Once again, she pursed her lips and pushed her tongue even further forward. This time, like a raspberry-blowing champion, Gertrude blew the loudest, longest raspberry the world had ever known.

"PFFFFFFFFFFFFFFFFFFFFFFFFFFFFFT!"

SUCCESS!

Despite now having his face covered in gorilla spittle, the boy couldn't help but laugh.

"HA! HA! HA!"

The stern-faced crowd began to chuckle too.

"HO! HO! HO!"

"Well played, boy!"

"The child is a marvel with animals!"

"This pair should be on the stage!"

Feeling ten-foot tall now, Eric was wondering if there was something else he could do? Could these raspberries be blown into something resembling a tune? There was only one way to find out.

The boy didn't know many songs. One he often sang in school assembly and had, in fact, sung that very morning was "Rule, Britannia!".

So, replaying the tune in his head, he began raspberrying* out the notes of the chorus.

"PFFFT! PFT! PFT! PFT!"

Eric then fell silent in the hope that Gertrude would follow his lead.

The gorilla tilted her head and looked at the boy as if he was barmy.

Undeterred by this, Eric persisted. The boy repeated himself.

"PFFFT! PFT! PFT! PFT!"

Gertrude tilted her head to the other side. Then a mischievous thought flashed across her eyes, and she pursed her lips together and pushed her tongue forward.

---

* *A real word that I have just made up. See your* **Walliamsictionary** *for the definition.*

"PFFFFFFFFFFFFFFFT!"

A long, low raspberry came out, once again covering the boy with gorilla spittle.

"Good luck with that one, lad!" snorted a voice from behind.

"Next you'll be teaching it to play the piano!"

"Or dance for the Royal Ballet!"

"HA! HA! HA!"

Eric could sense people ebbing away, but he was sure it was worth one more try.

"PFFFT! PFT! PFT! PFT!"

This time the most wondrous thing happened. Gertrude joined in!

"PFFFT! PFT! PFT! PFT!"

This little boy and this great ape were blowing raspberries to the tune of "Rule, Britannia!"...

Eric kept eye contact with Gertrude and nodded his head so she would keep time. He was pretty sure that she didn't know the song. Why would she? But she was picking it up very quickly.

"PFFFT! PFT! PFT! PFT!"

Soon, those that had shuffled away raced back to catch a glimpse of the show. More and more people joined, until there was a huge crowd gathered around the cage. Eric was concentrating so much on teaching the tune that he had managed to put them entirely out of his mind. Focusing on Gertrude, the pair reached the end of the chorus with one last big booming raspberry.

"PFFFFFFFFFFFFT!"

Instantly, the crowd broke into wild applause.

"MORE! MORE!"

"ENCORE!"

"PLAY US ANOTHER!"

The boy turned round. Because of the fuss, his face was now as red as a London bus.

"Well, I, er…"

Then at the back of the crowd he heard a voice. An angry voice. A voice he knew only too well… shouting his name.

"ERIC!"

CHAPTER 5

GRANNY SPITTLE

"ERIC!" the voice yelled again.

Now the boy blushed redder than a postbox.

The crowd looked around to see who this person was with the incredibly loud voice.

"Good afternoon, Grandma," replied the boy weakly.

"Don't you 'good afternoon, Grandma' me, boy! You are in almighty trouble! I ordered you to come straight home after school, but did you? Oh no! You had to come here to the zoo again, didn't you?"

There was no answer to that.

Eric was **BUSTED**.

The old lady batted the crowd out of the way with her ear trumpet.

BISH!

"OW!"

BASH!

"OOF!"

BOSH!

"ARGH!"

"Look at you, child!" she exclaimed, spotting that her grandson was covered in gorilla spittle. "Your face is FILTHY!"

Then the old lady did something Eric and all the children of all the world LOATHE. She spat on her handkerchief and began furiously rubbing away at his face.

Now Eric was covered in granny spittle instead of gorilla spittle. The boy wasn't sure which was worse.

As if that wasn't punishment enough, Grandma yanked him by one of his sticky-out ears.

"COME WITH ME!" she demanded. "I bet this was all your Uncle Sid's idea! That man is always filling your head with silly ideas!"

"Uncle Sid had nothing to do with it!" lied Eric.

"What did you say?" demanded the old lady, cupping the ear trumpet to her ear.

"UNCLE SID HAD NOTHING TO DO WITH IT!"

Grandma stared at the boy. "Bread and dripping!" she barked. "I bet there's another bombing raid tonight as soon as it's dark, which," she said, looking up at the sky, "is any moment now!"

With her free hand, Grandma hacked through the crowd with her ear trumpet as if it were a machete slashing through the jungle.

BISH!
"OUCH!"

BASH!
"ARF!"

BOSH!
"NOT AGAIN!"

Such was the commotion that more and more people began to gather: visitors, zookeepers and a stiff-looking man who was immaculately dressed in a morning suit complete with top hat. He tried to weave his way through the crowds.

"Please! Please! Some decowum, please!" he exclaimed. His voice was so achingly posh that his "r"s came out as "w"s. "Calm down, madam, please!"

"WHAT DID YOU SAY?" she shouted.

"I SAID 'CALM DOWN'!"

"All right! All right! No need to shout."

"Are you a little hard of heawing, madam?" asked the man, spotting the ear trumpet.

"A quarter past five," replied Grandma, checking her watch. "Who are you, anyway?" she added, putting the trumpet to her ear.

The man was taken aback by her tone. He spoke directly into the end of the trumpet. "I am Sir Fwedewick Fwown!"

"Fwedewick!" the old lady scoffed. "What kind of a name is that?"

"Fwedewick! It is a perfectly normal name for a gentleman."

"I think it's Frederick," hissed Eric, still wincing from the pain of having his ear pulled. "He runs the zoo."

"You are wight, boy. Fwedewick! And I am the zoo's diwector genewal!"

"The what?" she demanded.

"Diwector genewal!"

"Diwector genewal? What is a diwector genewal?"

"He is the director general, Grandma," said Eric.

"How many times do you need to be told?" bawled Frown. "Diwector genewal!"

"THERE'S NO NEED TO SHOUT, DEAR!" she shouted.

"I must politely ask you to leave the pwemises!"

"The pwemises?" she asked.

"Yes! The pwemises. With haste!"

"Don't you worry – we're going!" The lady marched off. On each of her steps, Gertrude blew a raspberry…

"PFT! PFT! PFT!"

...making it seem like the old lady was blowing off.

The crowd roared with laughter.

"HA! HA! HA!"

"Oh! My goodness gwacious!" exclaimed Sir Frederick. "Who taught my gowilla to do that? Was it you, big-eared boy?" he barked, nose to nose with Eric.

"Yes, sir," he confessed. "I was just trying to cheer up my friend after all the bombing last night. She was rocking backwards and forwards, and I was worried about her."

"So you taught her how to blow a waspbewy?"

"Yes, sir," replied the boy sorrowfully.

"This is a zoo! Not a circus!" thundered Frown.

"I couldn't agree more!" snapped Grandma. "You need to have a talk with the boy's great-uncle. He works here at the zoo. Sidney Pratt!"

"PWATT?"

"NO! PRATT!"

Grandma had dropped the zookeeper in a massive pile of elephant doo. Which, by a staggering coincidence, is exactly where Sid already was. However, Eric could hear that familiar clinking, clanking and clunking of the old man's tin legs in the distance.

CLINK! CLANK! CLUNK!

On spotting Sid, the boy shook his head as if to say, "Run!" Sadly, running was not the old man's strong point.

"Do you know this boy, Pwatt?" demanded Frown.

Eric shook his head.

"No?" lied the man.

"He's your great-nephew, Sidney!"

exclaimed Grandma. "I knew you were daft, but I didn't know you were this daft!"

"Oh, yes, I do, then," said Sid.

"Yes or no?" pressed Frown.

"A bit of both. No, I didn't know him, before he was born. But now I do, yes."

"I tell my grandson time and time again there's a war on! It's not safe! He needs to come straight home from school!" began Grandma. "But oh no! Sidney Pratt has other ideas! Wants the boy to be a zookeeper just like him! Shovelling doodahs all day! I bet he even sneaks the boy in here for free!"

Frown frowned. "Fwee? FWEE! Is this twue?"

Sid looked at Eric. The boy shook his head again, but the old man knew the game was up.

"Yes. It is twue, I mean true. My little Eric loves the animals, you see, and they love him…"

"Sidney Pwatt, wait for me in my office! You two, leave the zoo wight now."

"YOU WHAT?" barked Grandma, pushing the trumpet closer to her ear.

"LEAVE!"
"THERE'S NO NEED
TO SHOUT! And don't worry! We're going! I wouldn't come back into this stinky old place if you paid me!" huffed Grandma, yanking Eric's sticky-out ear. She'd made it stick out even further.

"OW!" exclaimed Eric as he was hauled away. He stole a look back at Sid, and then at Gertrude. The gorilla was sitting in her cage, having watched the entire scene. Although she couldn't speak human, Gertrude had clearly understood much of what had happened.

The boy was sad, so she was sad too.

The gorilla put her hand up to the cage. It was clear she didn't want her friend to go.

"HEE-HAW!" she cried after him, offering a little wave goodbye. Eric waved back, just before he was hauled off out of

sight

by his

ear.

"OWWW!"

CHAPTER | 6 |

MUM AND DAD

"STRAIGHT TO BED!" announced Grandma as she loomed over Eric at the kitchen table of her little terraced house. "Do you hear me? STRAIGHT TO BED!"

There was no chance of the boy not hearing her. She spoke so very loudly. "Straight to bed with no tea!"

"But—!"

"NO BUTS! YOU HAVE BEEN A VERY BAD BOY!"

Eric rose from the rickety chair and stomped up the stairs.

STOMP!

STOMP!

STOMP!

The first door was that of the tiny, dark, damp box room. It was full of Grandma's old junk, but was now Eric's bedroom. Feeling sorry for himself, he lay down on the bed, not even bothering to take off his school uniform. He closed his eyes. Holding on to the pillows, he imagined he was in the middle of a lovely family cuddle.

A **muddle.**

His dad had been killed six months before, during that summer at Dunkirk. Dad was one of thousands of British soldiers retreating from the Nazis across France. Dunkirk is the town on the northern coast of France from which the troops were being evacuated. However, many were killed as they tried to escape.

Including Private George Grout.

Dad had been a plumber – that's how he'd met his wife. He'd called round when her outside toilet was blocked. When war was declared in 1939, Dad proudly signed up to join the army. He was determined to do his bit to keep Britain safe from a Nazi invasion. However, his war would not be a long one. After surviving a number of fierce battles in France, tragedy struck at Dunkirk. The ship on which he was being evacuated, HMS *Grafton*, was torpedoed by a Nazi U-boat (or submarine).

Eric's mum was devastated when she received the telegram. Her darling husband was gone. She wept and wept and wept. Eric feared she might drown in her own tears, just as so many soldiers had drowned at Dunkirk. It was scary seeing his mum so sad. Would life ever feel normal again? Strangely there were still normal things to do, like eat your breakfast, brush your teeth or do your homework. After her husband's death, Mum was more determined than ever to help with Britain's war effort. She worked at a factory sewing parachutes for Spitfire pilots. However, tragedy was to strike Eric's short life again when a Nazi bomb destroyed the factory during a night shift.

No one got out alive.

One moment Mum was there, and the next she was gone. Just like with his dad, Eric didn't even have the chance to say goodbye. Nothing felt real to the boy any more. It was as if he were in a dream or, rather, a nightmare, where he was trapped underwater, and if he cried out nobody could hear him.

Now the boy was an orphan, it was hastily decided that Eric should go to live with his grandmother. The problem was that Grandma wasn't good with children.

Up there in the tiny box room of her house, Eric nestled himself between the two pillows on his bed. He dreamed they were his mum and dad. The pillows were cold and damp. Still, he shut his eyes. Maybe, just maybe, if he concentrated hard enough, he would find himself back in a perfect family **muddle.**

His daydream ended as the door swung open.

SWONK!

"I brought you some bread and dripping," announced Grandma.

Eric hadn't been expecting her, and hastily sat up on the bed, pushing the pillows to one side. He felt silly that the old lady might see him like this.

"Oh, thank you, Grandma," he chirped. He liked bread and dripping. Dripping was the fat from cooked meat, and it was tasty if you spread it on bread. He wolfed it down as the old lady perched next to him.

"I'm sorry I snapped at you, Eric," she said. "This war is hard. I lost a son; you lost a father. And, of course, you lost your mother too. I just couldn't bear it if any harm came to **you.**"

"I understand, Grandma," he spluttered, his mouth full of food. As Eric spoke, he sprayed breadcrumbs all over the floor. This made them both chuckle.

"Ha! Ha!"

Chuckling was not something they did much of together.

"You can have those crumbs in the morning for your breakfast!" said the old lady.

Eric wasn't sure if she was joking or not.

"Now, as soon as you finish your tea, I want you to go straight to sleep. We barely got a wink last night down in the underground."

The boy yawned. Grandma was right.

"And you need to be bright and breezy for school in the morning!"

Eric nodded weakly. Bright and breezy was never something he ever felt at school.

"Goodnight, Grandma."

"Porridge."

"NO, I SAID 'GOODNIGHT'!"

"NO NEED TO SHOUT, DEAR!"

"Goodnight, Grandma."

"Goodnight, boy."

The old lady wasn't one for hugs and kisses so she tapped the boy on the head as you might a pet instead.

TAP! TAP!

With that, she stood up and left the room, closing the door behind her.

SWONK!

Eric walked over to the grimy little window and looked up at the sky. It was dark and quiet right now. Eerily so.

Would the Nazi bombers return tonight?

There had been night after night of raids on London. So much so that it even had a name. The newspapers called it "the Blitz", after the German word for "lightning". Adolf Hitler's plan was to force Britain to surrender to the Nazis.

As Eric gazed across the frosted rooftops of London, his thoughts turned to Gertrude. The Nazi bombers were sure to strike again this evening. The gorilla had been left deeply distressed by last night's bombing raid. In his heart, Eric felt a deep longing to be with her. If he was by her side tonight, he was sure he could make things all right.

So the boy took a deep breath and summoned up all his courage. Then he slid open the window.

SHUNT!

Next, remembering exactly how Gertrude slid down her rope, he shimmied down the drainpipe. Then Eric ran off through the dark and empty streets of London.

CHAPTER 7

PENGUIN POOP

CLASSIFIED

LONDON ZOO was set in Regent's Park, one of the grandest outdoor spaces in the city. The park was closed at night, so Eric had to climb over the railings. Once inside, he circled the outer fence of the zoo for a while, searching for a way in. Ahead, he spotted a tall tree in the park, the branches of which drooped over into the zoo. Thinking again about how Gertrude would climb it, he scaled the tree trunk, using his hands and feet, just like the gorilla did. From the tree trunk, the boy shimmied across one of the branches on his bottom. But, as he scrambled further away from the trunk the branch thinned, and the inevitable happened.

CRACK!

The branch snapped!

Eric found himself tumbling through the air.

WHOOSH!

"ARGH!"
SPLOSH!

He was underwater!

Not just that, he could sense dozens of creatures swishing around him.

Had he fallen into a pool of piranhas?

Was he going to be gobbled alive?

Eric desperately swam to the surface and took a gasp of air.

GASP!

No. These were much bigger than piranhas. And far friendlier too.

They were PENGUINS!

"SQUAWK! SQUAWK! SQUAWK!"

The boy had plunged into the penguin pool!

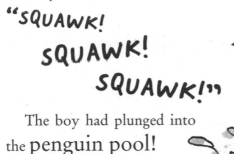

It had just been built and was more like a waterpark, with slides and a fountain. Perfect, if you were a penguin. Not so good if you were a boy.

The slippery birds played around Eric, pecking at him. One even perched on his head.

"Get off!" he said affectionately, as he guided the penguin back into the water. Eric swam to the edge of the pool and began clambering up the slide. But it was slippery, and he plunged back in the pool again.

WHOOMPH!

SPLOSH!

"SQUAWK! SQUAWK! SQUAWK!"

This time Eric swam over to the edge, and then he heard a familiar sound.

CLINK! CLANK! CLUNK!

It was Sid.

"What are you doing in there?" the old man called down.

"Taking a swim!" called Eric, trying to make light of the situation.

Sid huffed and shook his head. "Wait there!"

CLINK! CLANK! CLUNK!

There was silence for a moment before the old man returned with a long-handled net. It was the one he used for fishing out penguin poop.

"Hold on to this!"

Eric did as he was told, and Sid hauled him out of the water.

"You're soaking wet!" said the old man.

"That normally happens when you go for a swim," replied Eric.

"What are you doing here at the zoo so late? It's way after closing time!"

"I was worried about Gertrude. She looked so frightened today."

"She was, but you should be tucked up in bed by now, young man!"

"So should you!" said Eric.

This stopped the old man in his tracks. "I know, but I was sure there was going to be another bombing raid. We've had them night after night for weeks. I wanted to be here for all the animals!"

"Me too!" exclaimed the boy.

Sid looked up at the sky. "It's quiet up there in the clouds right now. You should go home!"

As if on cue, the air-raid siren wailed.

wooOHOOOO!

"I spoke too soon," hissed the old man. "Come with me."

Sid grabbed Eric by the hand and led him through the zoo.

CLINK! CLANK! CLUNK!

The zoo might have been in darkness because of the nightly blackout but it was noisier than ever. The air-raid warning had woken all the animals up.

"ROAR!" "HOOT!" "HISS!" "WHOOP!" "YELP!" "HONK!"

"Are we the only ones here?" asked Eric as he held his great-uncle's hand tightly.

"No, there'll be the nightwatchman, Batter. Or Corporal Batter as he demands to be known! We'll have to keep an eye out for him. He's the only one who's meant to be in the zoo after dark."

Eric could hear a distant humming sound. Next, a rumbling. Finally, there was a loud drone as the Nazi planes came right over their heads, flying in neat formation as they powered through the night sky.

Then the first bomb whistled through the air.

WHOOSH!

And the next.

WHOOSH!

And the next.

WHOOSH!

Then the explosions began.

KABOOM!

KABOOM!

KABOOM!

Lightning was striking all over London.

Searchlights scoured the sky, before big guns fired at the Nazi planes from the ground.

Fire-engine bells rang.

DING! DING! DING!

Eric could just make out the sounds of people screaming and shouting.

"ARGH!"

"HELP!"

"RUN!"

The boy's heart raced.

The noise.

The lights.

The debris.

KABOOM!

Another bomb exploded, even nearer than the last.

KABOOM!

And another!

KABOOM!

And another.

The elephants raised their trunks and hooted.

"HOO!"

The camels reared up on their back legs and moaned.

"WUHU!"

The lions leaped from rock to rock and roared.

"ROAR!"

KABOOM!

However, the saddest sound of all came from the gorilla's cage.

Gertrude's huge hands were covering her big ears as she tried to block out the booms of the bombs.

KABOOM!

At every explosion she let out a shriek…

"EEEHHH!"

…and rocked from side to side.

Eric broke away from the old man and hurled himself at the cage.

KABOOM!

"EEEHHH!"

"GERTRUDE!" cried the boy, but the gorilla wouldn't even open her eyes.

"GERTRUDE!"

KABOOM!

"RAISINS!" shouted Eric.

"You what?" spluttered Sid. It was clear that of all the things he was expecting the boy to shout at this point, "raisins" was a long way down the list.

"Raisins! They are her favourite! After bananas, of course, but you can't get bananas these days. A handful of raisins might just calm her nerves."

"You're right!" agreed Sid. "Clever boy! We'll make a zookeeper of you yet!"

The boy beamed. "Maybe one day! But where am I going to get raisins from at this time of night?"

KABOOM!

"The snack bar might have some!"

"But I don't have any money!"

"You won't need any money. It's closed!"

"Well, if it's closed, how am I going to get in?"

"You'll have to break in!"

Eric gulped. He'd never broken in anywhere, ever, and he was rather hoping to get through his whole life without doing so.

"Climb through the window!" shouted Sid over the noise. "Grab some raisins and run!"

CHAPTER | 8 |

FROZEN IN FEAR

The Nazi bombs were landing nearer and nearer to the zoo all the time.

KABOOM! KABOOOM! KABOOOOM!

Eric had been to the zoo so many times that even in the dark he knew his way around. In no time at all, he'd found the snack bar, climbed up on to a dustbin and forced a side window open. Next, he slid down inside and fumbled in the darkness to find a jumbo bag of raisins. Tempted though he was to take some sweets for himself, he resisted. Then, using a chair as a stepladder, he climbed up and out through the window, and leaped down on to the dustbin.

CLANG!

Eric glanced at the bag of raisins. There was a tear in it. He must have caught it on the little hook on the window frame. The boy did his best to stop the raisins falling out as he ran back to the gorilla's cage, bombs dropping all around.

KABOOOOOOOM! KABOOOOOOOM! KABOOOOOOOOM!

"I got the raisins, Uncle Sid!" he called out, breathless from the running.

The gorilla was still rocking, covering her ears, letting out a sad cry.

"EEEHHH!"

"Have you been eating them?" asked Sid, feeling that the bag was light.

"No, the bag got ripped and I dropped some on the way."

"A likely story!"

"It's true!"

The old man turned his attention to the gorilla. "Now, now, Gertrude! Come on, old girl! Your friend has a nice juicy raisin for you!"

Eric took one of the little treats out of the bag and pushed it through the metal bars.

KABOOOOOOOOO OOOOOOOOOOOOO oOoooooOooooooM!

This was the nearest explosion yet. Louder than all the others. They could feel the force of the blast. This bomb must have landed in Regent's Park. Soil sprayed everywhere, pelting the gorilla.

BIFF! BAFF! BOFF!

Poor Gertrude was scared out of her wits. She shrieked and shrieked and shrieked…

"EEEHHH! EEEHHH! EEEHHH!"

…as she leaped about her cage wildly.

"NOOO!" screamed the boy, terrified at what he saw.

Instead of taking the raisin as he'd hoped, the gorilla had bashed her head so hard against the cage that the wire had buckled.

BASH! BASH! BASH!

"Make her stop!" pleaded Eric.

Sid looked as worried as the boy. It was clear the old man had never seen the gorilla acting like this before.

"It's just a bad storm, Gertrude!" lied the zookeeper.

KkkKkkkKkkaAaaaAaaaa BBbbbbBbbBooOooooOoO MmmmMmmmmm!!!!!!!!!!

BASH! BASH! BASH!

"EEEHHH!"

This time Gertrude leaped to the middle of her cage and grabbed on to the rope tied to the metal bars at the top of her enclosure, and yanked with all her might.

"What's she doing?" cried Eric.

"She's trying to get out!" replied Sid.

The gorilla wrenched the rope so hard that the roof of her cage tore off from three sides.

TWONK!

Then it toppled into her cage.

KLUNCH!

It landed at an angle,
providing a ramp for
Gertrude to run
up, her huge feet
thudding on
the metal.

KLANK!

KLANK!

KLANK!

Eric and Sid looked on in a mixture of wonder and horror at the gorilla standing at the top of her cage. She was perfectly silhouetted by the full moon as she beat her chest and let out an almighty howl.

KABOOOOOOOOOOOOO OOOOOOOOOOOOOOOOO OOOOOOOOOOOOOOOOOO OOOOOOOOOOOOOOOOO OOOOOOOOOOOOOOOM!

Eric and Sid could feel the heat from the bomb. It must have landed inside the zoo itself. A tall tree in the picnic area exploded into flames.

WHOOF!

The heat was enough to sweep you off your feet.

Eric thought he was going to be burned alive.

The zoo lit up red and orange and yellow as black smoke darkened the sky.

Gertrude leaped down from the top of the cage and landed on the ground with a terrific THUD.

THOMP!

Eric stood frozen in fear as the huge creature lolloped over to him. She stared him right in the face, and he saw a look of terrible sadness in her eyes.

"Don't scream!" hissed Sid. "And don't make any sudden movements!"

The boy nodded slowly.

"If we keep still and quiet, then all should be fine…"

Gorillas were so **strong** they'd been known to tear a man's arm clean off.

Eric knew that.

But Gertrude was his friend. There had always been this special connection between the pair, even though the bars of the cage had kept them apart.

Until now.

They were now standing nose to nose. He could even feel her warm breath on his face.

Eric felt a strange mixture of joy and fear all at once. But the joy was stronger than the fear, and the boy smiled.

Gertrude loved to copy Eric, so she smiled back, flashing her teeth and those long fangs on each side of her mouth.

As Sid looked on and whispered, "Now be a good girl, Gertrude," the gorilla puckered up as if to give the boy a kiss. Eric had seen some films with lovey-dovey bits. He'd noticed how the grown-ups often closed their eyes when they kissed. So he did the same.

SPLURT!

But it wasn't a kiss. It was a raspberry!

"PFFFT!"

A big, wet raspberry. For the second time that day, Eric had gorilla spittle all over his face. But he didn't mind one bit.

"HA! HA! HA!" laughed the boy, and the gorilla joined in too.

"HUH! HUH! HUH!"

"You two!" chuckled Sid. "Now come on, Gertrude, let's get you back inside what's left of your cage."

With that, the man took the gorilla by the hand.

"Say goodnight, Eric," he said.

"Goodnight, Eric," repeated the boy. "WAIT! I am Eric!"

"I meant say goodnight to Gertrude, you great bozo!"

"Goodnight, Gertrude!"

"That's better," replied Sid, looking up at the sky. Once again, the Luftwaffe planes were nothing more than a distant hum. "Come on, old girl!"

"Let me help!" exclaimed the boy as he took Gertrude by her other hand.

Just then a gunshot rang out.

BANG!

A bullet whizzed just over their heads.

"EEEHHH!" screamed Gertrude.

The gorilla shook the pair from her hands, and they tumbled to the ground.

DOOF! DOOF!

"HUH!"

"EURGH!" they cried as Gertrude raced off into the darkness of the night.

KERTHUMP!

KERTHUMP!

KERTHUMP!

CHAPTER 9

BATTER

CLASSIFIED

The bombs might have stopped for the night, but the sound of gunshots startled all the animals in the zoo all over again.

"ROAR!"

"SNARL!" *"HOOT!"*

"WHOOP! WHOOP!"

"NEIGH!"

"What on earth do you think you are doing?" thundered Sid.

Eric had never seen the old man so angry.

He was shouting at a short, squat figure in the distance, who was now hurrying towards the pair.

"BATTER!" cried Sid.

"Corporal Batter to you!"

Corporal Batter was the nightwatchman for **LONDON ZOO**. He had been made a corporal in the First World War and had kept using the title. The rank was just above lance corporal, but below sergeant. An achievement, of course, but only a certain type of man would want to keep reminding people of it every single day, a hundred times a day, for the rest of his life.

A man like Batter.

The corporal's job was to make sure the animals didn't escape from their cages during the night. Since the Blitz had begun, there was every chance that one of the bombs could land in the zoo and destroy the cages and enclosures.

Then you might very well have:

…an escaped hippopotamus waddling down Oxford Street looking for a bargain…

"HOOT!"

…or a fugitive tiger leaping on the back of a double-decker bus…

"ROAR!"

...or a runaway rhinoceros charging towards 10 Downing Street to knock down the door of the prime minister himself!

THUMP!

When the Nazi bombing campaign began, **LONDON ZOO'S** resident vet, Miss Gnarl, had put down every single venomous snake or spider. There was a real chance these creatures could find their way into the homes of Londoners and kill them just like the bombs.

Imagine sitting on the toilet, and a huge, furry spider bites you on the bottom.

"URGH!"

Or lying in bed at night, and a snake slithers its way up your leg.

" AAAHHH!"

So Batter had been given the order that if a dangerous animal escaped from its cage during the night he could shoot it on sight. A gorilla more than fitted into this category. Sid and Eric were sure that Gertrude wouldn't hurt a flea. Well, that wasn't strictly true. If Gertrude found a flea in her fur, she would pluck it out and eat it. But this gorilla was more interested in blowing raspberries than harming anyone.

"I am… huh… huh…" huffed and puffed Corporal Batter as he finally reached the pair. The old soldier was out of breath.

"Well, out with it, man!" demanded Sid.

"I've… huh… got… huh… a huh…" spluttered Batter.

"What's a 'huh'?" asked Eric.

"I think he's just trying to get his breath back!" said Sid.

"I've… huh… got a… huh… stitch!" he uttered, clutching his tummy.

"Oh, boo-hoo!" exclaimed Sid. "You could have killed us!"

"I was aiming for the monkey!"

"A gorilla isn't a monkey – it's an ape!" protested the boy.

"Same difference!" snapped Batter.

"No, it isn't! And you can't shoot Gertrude. She's my friend!"

"I have my orders!" declared Batter.

With that, the old soldier cocked his rifle.

CLICK!

"Put that gun away, you fool!" exclaimed Sid, pushing its nose down.

"I will use my rifle whenever I want! It is me who is the war hero! Remember that, Private Sidney Pratt? Not you! You didn't last one day on the battlefields!"

Sid hung his head in shame. The man was right. His tin legs told that story.

Next, Batter turned his attention to the boy.

"And as for you! You are not even supposed to be here. A child at the zoo in the middle of the night! It is forbidden!"

"It's my fault, Batter," said Sid. "He's family!"

"Corporal Batter! Just wait until Sir Frederick Frown hears about this! Now stand aside! I have an escaped monkey to hunt!"

With that, he pushed the pair out of the way and marched off in the direction in which the ape had run.

Eric looked at Sid, tears welling in his eyes. "He's not really going to kill her, is he?"

"He's going to try!" said Sid.

"Then we need to stop him!"
cried Eric.

CLASSIFIED

CHAPTER | 10 |

A RUDE MAGIC TRICK

Finding an escaped gorilla in the dead of night is hard. The bombing raid had woken up every single animal in the zoo. Even though the Nazi planes were now heading back to Germany, the animals could not be calmed.

The parrots were squawking.

"SQUAWK!"

The lions were roaring.

"RoaR!"

And the elephants were hooting.

"HOO!"

So it was hard to know where in the zoo Gertrude might be, just from listening.

But Eric had an idea!

PING!

As soon as Batter had disappeared into the distance, Eric grabbed Sid by the hand.

"THIS WAY!" he hissed.

"HOLD UP!" said Sid, clanking along.

"Sorry, I forgot," said the boy.

"So do I sometimes, until they get rusty!"

CLINK! CLANK! CLUNK!

Moments ago, Eric had broken into the zoo's snack bar to fetch some raisins for Gertrude. As he'd climbed out of the snack-bar window, the bag of raisins had been ripped. The gunshot had spooked the gorilla, but if she'd followed her nose she may very well have found her way to the trail of the fruity treats on the ground. Eric and Sid retraced the boy's steps, but even using Sid's torch they couldn't see any. Perhaps the pigeons had got them?

Or maybe, just maybe, a much bigger creature?

The pair hurried past the flamingos, round the meerkats and along the warthogs to the snack bar. The snack-bar window that Eric had forced open was now flapping in the wind.

THWACK! THWACK! THWACK!

"You don't think she's in there, do you…?" asked Sid.

"Shush!" shushed the boy, before nodding his head.

The pair tiptoed over to the window. Sure enough, there was the gorilla, slumped on the floor amid a massive mess of food. There were bags and wrappers everywhere. Gertrude was alternating between swigging from a bottle of fizzy pop and munching on some jelly babies that had been scattered all over the floor.

"BURP!" burped the gorilla. It was as loud as thunder. It even shocked Gertrude. The gorilla had clearly never had fizzy pop before.

"HA! HA!" The pair at the window couldn't help but burst out laughing.

Gertrude looked up, startled.

"HURGH?" she gurgled.

"Shush, Gertrude! It's just us!" whispered Eric.

He dashed to the door.

"Locked!" he said.

"And I don't have the key!" replied Sid. "How are we going to get her safely back in her cage before Batter sees her?"

"We'll have to climb through the window!"

"At my age?" spluttered Sid.

"I'll help. Here, let me give you a leg up."

The old man sighed and muttered to himself. The boy couldn't work out what he'd said, but it sounded like one of those rude words grown-ups sometimes say that children aren't allowed to.

Eric put his hands together to form a little cradle and gestured for Sid to step on it. The boy had seen cowboys do this when mounting a horse in Westerns, and it looked like a doddle! However, Eric was not a strapping cowboy, and neither was Sid. The man certainly was not helped by having battered old tin legs. So, after a wobbly start, poor Sid ended up falling through the open window, the back of his trousers getting caught on the hook.

WHOOSH!

Like a magic trick, a RUDE magic trick, the old man's trousers and undercrackers* were yanked back as he slid downwards.

"ARGH! ME BOTTY!" he exclaimed, and he landed in a crumpled heap on the floor. Eric should really have had his serious face on at this moment, all kind and concerned, but he just couldn't. Instead he burst out laughing.

"HA! HA! HA!"

Now, laughter is infectious. Either that or gorillas find wrinkly old bottoms funny, because Gertrude burst out laughing too.

"HEE! HEE! HEE!"

If you have never seen a gorilla laugh, it is a wonderful sight to behold!

They rock their heads back, they bare their teeth and thump the floor.

THUMP! THUMP!

"HEE! HEE! HEE!"

---

* It means underpants. Please see your **Walliamsictionary**.

"HELP ME!" cried Sid, still lying on the floor.

The boy unhooked the man's trousers, and then climbed through the window. He helped him up...

CLINK! CLANK! CLUNK!

...and slowly the pair approached the gorilla.

"BURP!" she burped again.

The boy caught a waft.

"POO!" he moaned. "Gorilla burps smell BAD!"

"Wait until you smell what comes out of the other end!" remarked the old man. "That really pongs!"

"HA! HA!" laughed Eric. Anything to do with bottom burps always made him chuckle. "So how are we going to get Gertrude back to her cage?"

"Mmm," said Sid, surveying the scene. The gorilla looked perfectly content gulping and guzzling away.

"BURP!"

This one was pongy enough to sweep you off your feet.

"I've got an idea!" exclaimed the boy. "If Gertrude followed a trail of raisins here, she might just follow a trail back!"

"BINGO!"

The boy beamed with pride, before looking around

the snack shop for more bags of raisins. Unfortunately, Gertrude had already demolished all but one. Eric seized the last remaining bag and waggled it in front of the gorilla's face.

"Gertrude!" he said in a sing-song voice that everyone adopts when talking to animals. "Yummy scrummy raisins!"

"Let me see if I can get this door open!" said Sid. He didn't want to risk his trousers coming down and the world seeing his bottom again. The man found the spare key on the shelf and unlocked the door.

CLICK!

"DONE IT!" announced Sid, turning back to Eric and Gertrude.

"RAISINS!" called out the boy. "Nice juicy raisins!"

With that, he scattered some raisins in the gorilla's path.

Just as Eric had thought, Gertrude stood up, and began lolloping towards them, picking each one up and munching it down.

MUNCH! MUNCH! MUNCH!

Eric smiled. His plan was going exactly to plan! He scattered some more raisins all the way to the door. Sid stood proudly saluting by the door, ready to open it like a doorman at a posh hotel.

"This way, madam!" he chirped as he swung the door open.

What none of them realised was that standing on the other side of the door was... BATTER!

The old soldier squeezed the trigger on his rifle, ready to fire...

CHAPTER 11

BANG!

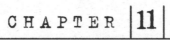

"NOOOOO!" screamed Eric, jumping between Gertrude and the rifle. He knocked the gun out of Batter's hands as he did so.

BANG!

A shot rang out. The bullet exploded through the snack-bar roof.

BOOF!

"WHOOP!" cried the gorilla.

Gertrude was terrified and charged at Batter.

Their heads clonked together.

DOINK!

Both fell to the ground, knocked out cold.

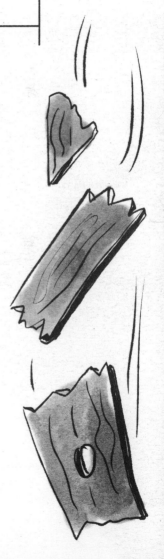

"What on earth did you think you were doing, boy?" shouted Sid.

"I was just trying to save Gertrude!" protested Eric.

"You could have got yourself killed! Killed!"

"I'm sorry."

"And now we are in deep, deep doo-doo!"

Eric looked down at the pair sprawled on the ground.

"Do you think they are all right?" he asked.

"Gertrude or Batter?" asked Sid.

"Well –" the boy hesitated – "I was thinking of the gorilla!"

"Come on! We need to sort both of them out!"

That is what they did. They found a large wheelbarrow, normally used to ferry dung around the zoo.

"Ladies first!" announced Sid, and with great effort they lifted Gertrude into it. She was wheeled back to her cage, which they thought was the safest place for her despite the damage to the roof.

First, Sid and Eric untied the rope, and then attached it to the top of the roof. Next, using the branches of a nearby tree as a pulley, they hoisted the top of the cage back into position. Then, to stop it from falling down again, they tied it off round the trunk of a tree. To hide the damage, they put some hay and twigs around the top of the cage so you couldn't see where the roof had been torn off.

Finally, they wheeled Gertrude into her cage, gently lifted her out of the wheelbarrow and set her down on a bed of straw.

The gorilla snored away.

"ZZZ! ZZZZ! ZZZZZ!"

"She looks peaceful when she sleeps," remarked Eric.

"Let's get out of here before she comes to," replied Sid. "That was a nasty bump on the head! She might wake up in a foul mood!"

"Gertrude's never in a foul mood."

"No, but we'd be safest on the other side of this cage. Come on!"

The boy gave his friend a goodnight kiss on her forehead, just like his mum and dad used to do to him.

"Sleep tight!" he said.

By the time they were out of her cage, dawn was rising over the zoo. With the sun up, Eric and Sid could see plumes of thick, black smoke rising up all over London. This must have been one of the worst nights of bombing in the war so far. Night after night, building by building, London was being flattened. If the explosions of the bombs didn't bring death and destruction, then the blazes they caused would.

So many buildings in London would now be nothing but a blackened shell. Looking up at the sky above inked with smoke, Eric felt lucky to be alive. Although he was meant to be tucked up in bed at his grandma's house, perhaps the zoo was the safest place to be, after all.

Now Eric and Sid had to act fast. Soon, more and more

people who worked at the zoo would be arriving. They would be asking questions as to why the nightwatchman was sprawled out on the ground.

When they finally got back to the snack bar to deal with Batter, the man and his rifle were nowhere to be seen.

"He's gone!" called out Eric.

"Oh no I haven't!" said Batter as he stepped out of the shadows.

"You two are in **ginormous** trouble!"

CHAPTER 12

DEEP DOO-DOO

CLASSIFIED

After being locked in Batter's shed for what seemed like hours, the pair were marched to the zoo director's office. It was an oak-panelled room, with oil paintings and busts of the previous zoo directors. The list of bad things Sid and Eric had done was long. As Sir Frederick Frown listed them one by one, all the boy could think about was that he really needed a pee.

"Bweaking into the zoo duwing the night. Bwinging a child into the zoo without authowisation. Attacking a member of staff. Letting a dangewous animal woam the zoo at night. And, last but not least, bweaking into the snack bar and stealing waisins!"

Eric couldn't help but smirk at Frown's posh way of pronouncing words.

"The impudence!" thundered Frown. "Boy, you deserve a good old-fashioned thwashing!

And why do you smell of penguin?"

Eric's clothes were still damp. "I fell in the penguin pool."

"Fell in the penguin pool! What a widiculous thing to do! You could have dwowned! I despair. I weally do. Where, pway, are your mother and father in all this?"

The boy hung his head. Nothing seemed funny any more. "Both died in the war, sir."

The man softened. "I am so vewy sowwy to hear that."

"Thank you, sir."

"But goodness gwacious. This is not good. Not good at all. Orphan or not, this is the second time you have

been in twouble at my zoo in twenty-four hours!"

"Sorry, sir."

"Mmm, but it's not you I blame for all this. You have been led astway by this man here."

He jabbed his finger in Sid's direction. Now it was the old man's turn to hang his head.

"Sorry, sir," muttered Sid.

"Sowwy isn't good enough. You have been a keeper here at the zoo for longer than anyone. Not once, but twice you have bwoken that bond of twust. You have no wight to be in the zoo duwing the night!"

"I was only trying to take care of all the animals during the bombing raid!"

"It is not your job to do that, Pwatt. Batter here is—"

"Corporal Batter, if you please, sir," corrected the corporal, who was standing in the corner with a smug look on his face.

Frown rolled his eyes. "Corpowal Batter here has orders of how to deal with animals who escape duwing the night. And you pwevented him fwom doing that. Imagine if we had a gowilla wunning wiot thwough the stweets of London?"

Eric began imagining the scene.

GERTRUDE READING A
NEWSPAPER ON A BENCH
IN HYDE PARK

GERTRUDE SCALING
NELSON'S COLUMN

GERTRUDE CLINGING ON
TO THE HANDS OF THE
CLOCK FACE ON BIG BEN

GERTRUDE WAVING FROM THE
DOORWAY OF 10 DOWNING STREET
AS IF SHE WERE THE PRIME
MINISTER

GERTRUDE STANDING ON THE DOMED ROOF OF ST PAUL'S CATHEDRAL

GERTRUDE DRIVING A LONDON TAXI CAB

GERTRUDE FEEDING THE PIGEONS IN TRAFALGAR SQUARE

GERTRUDE TAKING TICKETS ON THE TUBE

GERTRUDE SIPPING AFTERNOON TEA AT THE SUPER-POSH CLARIDGE'S HOTEL

GERTRUDE PLAYING CROQUET WITH KING GEORGE VI IN THE GARDENS OF BUCKINGHAM PALACE

The boy smiled to himself. A gowilla wunning wiot seemed like awfully good fun!

"It would be chaos!" concluded Frown. "That gowilla is a gwave danger to the public!"

"I know her better than any of you! Gertrude's a big softie! She's harmless!" protested the boy.

"That gorilla could rip your arms clean off!" bawled Batter.

"Then it would be Eric who'd be 'armless!" quipped Sid.

"Is that supposed to be funny?" demanded Frown.

"Just trying to lighten the mood, sir!"

"Well, don't. This isn't a laughing matter. That gowilla destwoyed its cage! It has no place in my zoo! And as for you, boy, you are a child – you don't know the first thing about these cweatures!"

This stung Eric. He might not have been an animal expert with all the facts and figures, but he did have a special connection with them. Especially his dearest darling Gertrude.

"Batter, fetch the vet, the delightful Miss Gnarl. She can put down the gowilla!"

"Very good, sir!" replied Batter with a self-satisfied grin as he left Frown's office.

"NOOOOOO!" screamed Eric.

"Please, please, please! I beg you!" pleaded Eric. "You can't put Gertrude down! She's my best friend in the world!"

The boy burst into tears.

"I wun this zoo, not you! It is the only solution for **that beast!**" thundered Frown.

He checked the time on his gold pocket watch that nestled in his waistcoat.

"Boy! You should be in school soon! Now huwwy home. I need to have words with your gweat-uncle!"

Sid gulped.

"GULP!"

He knew what was coming.

"What's going to happen to him?" asked the boy, wiping away his tears with his soggy sleeve.

"That is none of your business. Now please leave the pwemises at once. And this time don't come back. I never, ever, EVER want to see you in my zoo again! You have been warned, you wascal!"

"I can't let you hurt Gertrude! I won't!"

At that moment, a tall, broad lady in a crumpled white coat marched into the room. Batter, who was pacing behind, looked positively tiny next to her. She wore a monocle over one of her eyes, both as dark as night. Her greying hair was arranged like a bird's nest. When she grinned ghoulishly, she revealed the blackest teeth you ever did see. In her hand she held a syringe with a strange purple liquid inside.

"Ah, good morning, Miss Gnarl!" chirped Frown.

Miss Gnarl merely growled in reply. **"GRRR!"**

The startling sound made Eric tremble.

"It is with some sadness that I command you to put down

the gowilla!" announced Frown.

"GRRR! GR! GRRRR!" she replied.

"What did she say?" asked Frown, frowning.

"Let me translate for you, sir!" offered Batter. "I have learned to speak Gnarl. She said, **'It would be a great pleasure, Sir Frederick!'**"

"Jolly good!" replied Frown, although from his face it looked as if he wasn't convinced this was what she'd really said. "Thank you!"

The vet held her syringe aloft, her dark eyes widening with delight. She turned on the heel of her boot to make her way to the door.

"NOT YET!" ordered Frown. "It will have to be done tonight as soon as the zoo closes. We wouldn't want the public to see. Might upset the childwen."

Miss Gnarl didn't look convinced as she shook her head and growled again. **"GRRR! GR! GGGR!"**

"What did she say?" asked Frown.

"Miss Gnarl says, **'But I like upsetting the children, sir,'**" translated Batter.

"I am well aware of that, Miss Gnarl, but that is my order! As soon as the zoo closes tonight, you may put down the gowilla!"

"NO!" cried Eric. "I beg you! NO!" He sank to his knees in desperation, his eyes stinging with tears. "Please don't do this! You can't kill Gertrude! She's the kindest, gentlest animal in this zoo! If she could speak human, I know she'd promise never to escape from her cage ever again!"

"I can't listen to any more of this nonsense!" declared Frown. "Boy! I want you out of my zoo fowever!"

"BUT – BUT – BUT—!"

"NOW!" he barked.

Sid nodded for Eric to go. The boy hung his head. He couldn't bear to look at Frown, Batter or the terrifying Gnarl. He traipsed out of the room, utterly defeated, and closed the door behind him. To his surprise, the corridor was empty. So he lingered there, placing his ear up against the keyhole.

"Sidney Pwatt!" announced Frown grandly. "You are fired fwom this zoo!"

"But, sir…" pleaded the man, "I have given my whole life to this zoo!"

"No 'buts'!"

"No one can take care of the animals like I do!"

"If your idea of taking care of these cweatures is

letting them escape from their cages while a child is on the pwemises, then you should never be let near a zoo again!"

"SIR?"

"Batter! Escort this man off the pwemises at once!"

"With pleasure, sir!" snarled Batter.

"Miss Gnarl, I will see you the moment the zoo closes!"

"GRRR! GRRRR! GRR! GRRRRRR! GGGRRRR! GR! GGGGGR! GRRRRRRRRR! GR! GRRRRRRRRRRRRRRRRRRR!"

"What did she say?" asked Frown.

"'Yes!'" translated Batter.

The boy heard the sound of Sid's tin legs clanking towards the door.

CLINK! CLANK! CLUNK!

Eric darted down the corridor and hid round a corner. From there, he watched in sorrow as Sid was marched out of the building by Batter.

Left to his own devices, Eric tiptoed off to see his friend. Was this to be his final glimpse of her? It was still early, and the zoo hadn't opened to visitors yet. As the mist cleared, he found her cage.

The gorilla was stirring.

"Gertrude!" hissed the boy. **"GERTRUDE!"**

On hearing her friend's voice, the gorilla sat straight up. She looked funny, all covered in straw. Spotting the boy, she smiled, oblivious to the terrible fate that awaited her.

"HEE!" exclaimed the gorilla.

"Shush!" shushed the boy, putting his finger to his lips. He didn't want Batter to find him here.

The gorilla put her sausage finger to her lips too. The boy couldn't help but smile.

"I love you, Gertrude. I really do," said the boy.

The gorilla tilted her head, as if she were trying to understand.

Eric tried again. This time he mimed. He touched his heart, and then put his hand up to the cage.

To his surprise, the gorilla did the same. She put her hand on her heart, and then met his hand on the other side of the metal.

As their palms touched, tears beaded in the boy's eyes.

"This isn't goodbye. It can't be. I will find a way, Gertrude. Trust me. I'll find a way."

125

Fumbling in his trouser pocket, he found one last raisin. He pushed it through the bars.

The gorilla took it, shook her head and passed it back to him. The boy opened his mouth and she pushed the raisin in.

The boy chewed it and smiled. She smiled too.

Then a look of worry crossed the gorilla's face, and at that moment Eric felt a firm hand on his shoulder.

"YOU! OUT!"

The boy turned round. It was Batter.

Without another word, he marched the boy away from the cage in the direction of the exit. Eric turned back towards Gertrude, with his hand on his heart again. Gertrude being Gertrude did the same.

It couldn't be the last time Eric ever saw her.

It just couldn't.

CHAPTER | 14 |
EAR TRUMPET

Corporal Batter hurled Eric out of the exit gate as if he were nothing more than a sack of rubbish.

HUMPH!

"AND DON'T COME BACK!"

barked Batter as the boy scrambled to his feet.

Eric said nothing. He dashed all the way home. His grandmother would be waking up soon, and she'd be worried about him if she didn't find him tucked up in bed in the morning.

However, as the boy turned the corner on to the street where he lived, he noticed something strange. So strange that at first he thought he might be having a dream. Or, rather, a **nightmare.** The little terraced house that he shared with his grandmother just **wasn't there.**

Instead, there was a smouldering wreck and a gap in the row of houses. The roof had fallen in, and so had most of the first floor. The ground was a mess of bricks, tiles and furniture.

Was that the old tin bath? Or the armchair? Or the sideboard?

All were upside down and blackened by fire.

A fire engine was at the scene, but the firemen were packing up their hose. There was nothing more that could be done. A crowd of people stood and stared. Some had their arms round each other, some were sobbing, others were muttering words of sadness.

"Poor old Mrs Grout."

"She'd lived there for fifty years. She didn't deserve this."

"It would have all been over in a flash. Boom! She wouldn't have known what hit her."

"I curse that Mr Hitler! I would biff him on the nose if I had half a chance!"

"It's the boy I feel most sorry about."

"Oh yes, the boy! He'd only just moved in!"

"That's right! Her grandson, Eric."

"What was he? Ten? Eleven?"

"Poor little soul. He had his whole life ahead of him."

"And he'd lost his mummy and daddy too.

Unfortunate wretch."

"They're all together in heaven now."

It was only when Eric reached them that he realised they were talking about him. The boy felt the strangest feeling. It was as if he were at his own funeral. They must think he was buried under the rubble of the house with his poor grandmother – which he would have been had he not sneaked out of bed to help Sid at the zoo.

He spotted Grandma's ear trumpet amongst the rubble.

It had been crushed, like everything else.

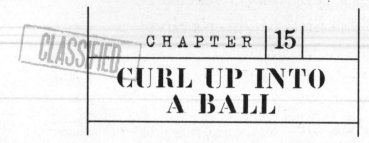

CHAPTER 15

CURL UP INTO A BALL

Eric felt sick to his stomach. He should have been at home with Grandma. Maybe if he had, he might have been able to save her. The old lady was more than a little deaf. She must not have heard the air-raid warning. The boy couldn't help but burst into floods of tears. Now he had not just lost his father and mother in this wretched war, but his grandmother too. Next, he was about to lose his best friend in the world. Eric sobbed so hard that the onlookers turned and stared.

"It's him!"

"It's Eric!"

"It's a miracle!"

"Thank goodness!"

"He's saved!" they exclaimed.

The boy found himself being crowded around, cuddled and then hoisted high up in the air as if he were a prize at the fair. Being shy, Eric hated it.

"The little blighter's alive!"

"The boy's survived!"

"Praise the Lord!"

"You must come and live with me!"

"No, me!"

"I will take the boy in! And I have a cat! He likes animals!" said an old man.

"Loves them! I have a rabbit! We are going to have it for dinner soon, but he can stroke it until we do!" exclaimed a tall lady.

"He can live with me in my sweet shop!" suggested a portly man. "I'll have to talk him through all the special offers first, though!"

The boy tried to smile. These grown-ups were doing their best to be nice. But all Eric wanted was to curl up into a ball and be left alone forever.

Just then, a pair of policemen plodded over.

"Excuse me," began one firmly, "the boy needs to come down to the station with us! We will be the ones in charge of finding him a home."

With that, Eric was lowered to the ground.

"Was this your house, lad?" asked the policeman.

He nodded, sniffing back the tears.

"What's your name?"

"Erm, its Eric. Eric Grout."

The policeman held out his hand. "Come along, then, Eric Grout. We'll look after you."

"Don't you worry," said the other policeman. "We'll find a nice home for you."

"Best to get you out of London," said the first. "It's not safe in the city for a little one like you. There are plenty of families out in the countryside who would take you in. I am sure of it!"

Eric didn't want to be sent to live with strangers far away. He had to escape and save Gertrude.

The boy said nothing. But, as they turned a street corner, he shook free of their grip

and made

a run

for it...

CHAPTER 16

CLASSIFIED

STOP THAT BOY!

One of the policemen blew his whistle…

TOOT-TOOT!

…while the other shouted, "STOP THAT BOY!"

Eric darted down the road as the policemen gave chase. Londoners had emerged from the underground or their bomb shelters. They were gathered in groups inspecting the terrible damage from the night's bombing.

Rubble was being searched for survivors.

People were calling out the names of loved ones.

"GRANDAD? GRANDAD?"

Others fell to their knees and wept to see everything they'd worked for all their lives destroyed.

But most looked around as they heard the police whistle and the cry of, "STOP THAT BOY!"

Why did he need to be stopped?

Times were hard, and it had been known for some to steal from the bombed-out homes, or even the bodies of the dead. Was the boy a thief?

Soon, some folks were joining in the chase.

"STOP THAT BOY!" came more and more cries.

Eric was frightened. All he could think to do was run faster and faster and dodge out of the way of the sea of arms reaching out to grab him.

"GET HIM!"
"STOP HIM!"
"CATCH HIM!"

More police whistles sounded.

TOOT-TOOT!!

Suddenly, it seemed as if the whole of London were after him.

Still Eric kept running.

He was exhausted from being up all night, but somehow his little legs kept powering him along.

Now he was running across roads, dodging out of the way of buses and taxis.

Ahead of him was London Bridge, which stretched out across the River Thames. Behind him, the policemen and the mob were gaining on him. Up ahead, Eric could see a trio of policemen on bicycles pedalling in his direction. The policemen leaped off their bicycles...

CLATTER!

...and blocked the boy's path.

Now he was trapped. Eric was in BIG TROUBLE for running away from the policemen. He had to flee. But there was nowhere to go.

The boy held on to the balustrade of the bridge and looked out across the Thames.

Chugging under the bridge was a barge loaded with hundreds of cardboard boxes.

The angry grown-ups were getting closer and closer.

Eric climbed on to the top of the railings.

The mob stopped, forming a semicircle round him.

"DON'T DO ANYTHING STUPID, SON!"

shouted the first policeman.

Eric only had seconds to make his decision. Any moment now, the boat would have passed.

Could he?

Eric closed his eyes. Once again, he pictured how Gertrude leaped from one place to another. So, with all his strength, Eric pushed off with his feet.

wHOOSH!

"NOOO!" someone shouted.

It was too late.

Eric was sailing through mid-air…

CHAPTER | 17 |

SID'S SECRET

CLASSIFIED

DOOSH!

Eric landed on the cardboard boxes on the boat.

On London Bridge, whistles blew.

TOOT-TOOT!

Shouts could be heard.

"STOP THAT BOAT!"

"SOMEBODY DIVE IN AFTER HIM!"

"DON'T LET HIM GET AWAY!"

But they were deafened by the sound of the barge's engine as it powered along the Thames.

CHUGGER! CHUGGER! CHUGGER!

Soon the bridge and all those on it were in the distance.

Eric lay down on one of the boxes, resting at last after what had been the most dramatic of nights. Grandma was gone forever. He couldn't let the same fate befall

Gertrude. He had a matter of hours to save her.

Soon Eric could feel the barge slowing as it entered the port. He hid between a gap in the boxes, and as soon as the barge reached the dock he leaped off. The port was bustling with dockers hard at work, and no one paid much attention to this little stowaway.

Now Eric was in a distant and unfamiliar part of East London.

The boy had to find his Uncle Sid. With the old man's help, he was sure they could save Gertrude.

In no time, Eric spotted the nearest underground station. Without money to pay for a train ticket, he had no choice but to slip through the barrier. When the ticket inspector called after him…

"HEY! COME BACK HERE!"

…he leaped on to the stair rail and slid down it on his bottom.

WHOOSH!

He sped past Londoners trudging up the steps, laden with blankets, pillows and the like after spending the night on the platform. Eric leaped aboard the first train and sped across the city.

It was strange that for all the years Eric had known his Uncle Sid he'd never once visited his house. No one had. It was something of a family joke. You never went to Uncle Sid's house; he always came to yours. This made the boy imagine that the old man might be hiding something.

Was his house stupidly small? Or horrendously messy? Or did he hate people using his toilet?

Soon the boy was going to discover Sid's secret.

Although he'd never been there, Eric remembered the old man's address from writing Christmas and birthday cards to him. So, studying the map in the train carriage, he found the right stop, Clapham Common, and hopped off.

Blinking in the bright sunlight, Eric discovered it was just a short walk from the station to Sid's house. Up in the sky, he could see one of London's many barrage balloons bobbing about. These huge balloons were tethered to the ground all over the city. Their job was to impede enemy aircraft, but, judging by the devastation of last night's bombing raid, they hadn't made a big difference.

Sid lived in an impossibly narrow terraced house, pretty much the same as every impossibly narrow terraced house on the street.

That was the outside.

The inside, however, was a completely different story.

Eric knocked on the battered old front door.

KNOCK! KNOCK!

"I am not in!" came a cry from the other side of the

door. It was Sid all right and, by all accounts, he was very much in.

Eric knocked again.

KNOCK! KNOCK!

"I am out!"

"No, you're not!" called the boy.

"Yes, I am!"

"Uncle Sid! It's me! Eric!"

There was silence for a moment.

Then came the sound of tin feet clanking on the floor.

CLINK! CLANK! CLUNK!

The letterbox opened.

SHUNT!

"What are you doing here?" hissed Sid through the letterbox.

"I've come to see you."

"I don't accept visitors. Ever!"

There was a strange honking sound in the background.

HONK!

"What was that?" asked Eric.

"What was what?" replied Sid, pretending he hadn't heard anything.

"That sound!"

"I didn't hear anything!"

HONK! HONK!

"There it is again!"

"Oh, that."

"Yes, that!"

"Just my bottom honking! I had some dried prunes for breakfast."

"I know the sound of your bottom honking only too well and it doesn't sound like that!"

"I'm so sorry, Eric. It's not a good time!"

"Please. I have nowhere else to go."

"Don't be silly. What about your granny?"

"She's gone."

The next thing Eric heard was a bolt being unbolted and a lock being unlocked.

SHUNT!
CLICK!

The door opened, and Sid stood there with his arms

wide open. The boy walked towards him, and they embraced. The pair stood and held each other tight.

No words were necessary.

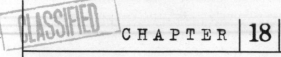

CHAPTER 18

HONK! HONK! HONK!

After a while, the old man broke the silence. "I am so, SO sorry," he spluttered through tears.

"Thanks," sniffed Eric. "The whole house was blown up in the night."

"Poor old dear. I know we didn't always see eye to eye, but she did her best to look after you."

"I know. She tried."

"She loved you, even though she didn't know how to show it."

"I know."

"She didn't deserve for her life to end like this."

"No one does," agreed the boy.

"Deaf as a post, she was! She didn't stand a chance."

"It's all my fault!" exclaimed Eric. "I should have been there!"

"You mustn't say that! This blasted war isn't your fault."

"I should have woken her up when the air-raid warning sounded."

"If you'd been there, chances are you'd be dead too."

The boy gulped.

"GULP!"

The old man was right.

"With Granny gone, I've got no one now," he blubbered.

"You've got me!" exclaimed the old man. "You'll always have me."

The pair hugged each other even tighter.

"Thank you, Uncle Sid."

HONK! HONK! HONK!

"There's that sound again!" exclaimed Eric.

"Come in, come in, and let's shut the door."

They did so, and as soon as they were inside and away from prying eyes and ears Sid said, "Look, you need to promise not to tell anybody."

"Promise not to tell anybody what?"

"Well, you need to promise first. I can't tell you before you've promised!"

"I promise!" said Eric.

"Come with me," whispered Sid, and he led the boy down the narrow hall,

"so you can meet my

secret family…"

PART TWO

BLOOD, SWEAT, TOIL AND TEARS

CHAPTER 19

A KINGDOM OF CREATURES

CLASSIFIED

"Secret family?" spluttered Eric. What on earth was the old man talking about?

"Shush!" shushed Sid as he opened the narrow door to his kitchen.

Inside that little room was a kingdom of creatures.
Eric's eyes widened with delight as he saw:

A one-winged parrot perched on a kettle.

"SQUAWK!"

A baby elephant with an incredibly short trunk.

"HOO!"

A blind seal swimming up and down in a tin bath.

"HOO!"

A giant tortoise with a wicker basket for a

shell crawling across the floor.

MUNCH!

A one-legged flamingo toppling over in the corner.

DONK!

A crocodile with no teeth scuttling under a table.

SNAP!

And last but not least a one-armed baboon with the most enormous bright red bottom you've ever seen climbing up the shelves.

"HOOT! HOOT!"

Eric's mouth fell open. He was speechless.

"This is why I can't have anyone over for tea!" announced Sid.

"Have they all got names?" asked the boy eagerly.

"Yes, of course they've all got names! Eric, please allow me the pleasure of introducing them to you."

The boy beamed with anticipation.

"This is Parker the parrot. You can shake her wing. Be gentle, though, as she's only got **one!**"

Eric reached out and took Parker's one wing in his hand.

"How do you do?" he said.

"How do you do?" squawked the parrot. **"How do you do?"**

"She speaks!" exclaimed the boy.

"Yes. Lots of parrots do!"

"Parrots do! Parrots do!" came a squawk.

"She talks all right," began Sid. "She likes to repeat whatever you just said, so it's not always the most exciting conversation."

"Exciting conversation!"

"I love her!" said Eric.

"Me too! She's the first one I got. So she'll always be special."

"Always be special!"

"That you will be," said Sid, tickling the parrot under

her chin. "This is Ernie!" he continued, shaking the baby elephant by his unusually short trunk.

"Isn't Ernie going to grow?"

"That he is. I fear he's going to eat me out of house and home one day. Here, grab that apple," said Sid, pointing over to a shelf.

The boy took it, nearly tripping over the crocodile as he did so.

"Ernie's trunk is too short for him to feed himself. So you have to do it by hand. You can feed him if you like."

Eric lifted up the apple to the baby elephant and placed it in his mouth.

MUNCH!

"He'll be your best friend forever now!" chirped Sid.

The boy patted the elephant on his side before giving him a hug. "I hope so. I love him."

"Don't make the others jealous!" said Sid. "Come on, you've got plenty more friends to meet!"

One by one, Sid introduced Eric to all the animals in the room.

"Sassy the seal!"

SPLISH! SPLASH! went the seal in the tin bath. "She's as blind as a bat. Well, blinder, really, as bats have that sonar thingummyjig, so we need to take very good care of her."

"I will," said Eric, running his fingertips gently along the seal's soft fur. Although the animal couldn't see the boy, she could feel him. A smile crept across her face.

"HONK!"

Just then the tortoise loomed into view, carrying the wicker basket on its back.

"What happened to his shell?" asked Eric.

"It got smashed to pieces when poor Totter here was transported all the way from Galapagos on a boat. He's now got my laundry basket for a shell."

Eric noticed how the basket was tied underneath the

tortoise with string. He patted the creature on its head and said, "Poor thing."

"Totter's a fighter. He'll keep tottering along until way after we're gone. Some tortoises live well past a hundred!"

DOOF!

The flamingo toppled over again.

"Why does the flamingo keep falling over?" asked Eric. "I thought flamingos could stand on one leg!"

"They can!" replied Sid, righting her. "But they do use their other leg for balance. So, if you're born with just the one leg, like Florence here, you can't help toppling over."

DOOF!

"Oh, there she goes again!" he continued.

Eric reached out and stroked her side as she lay on the floor. "Her feathers are so soft," he remarked.

"Yes! Perfect for dusting."

"You what?"

"I use her leg as a pole, and then I pick her up and dust the top of the cupboards!"

Sid couldn't help but smirk.

"You are JOKING!"

"Ha! Ha! Of course I'm joking! I wouldn't do a thing to hurt poor Florence," said Sid, leaning her up against the wall.

"Maybe she needs some crutches to help her get around."

"That's a good idea, Eric! Or some tin ones like me! I have tried a few things for Florence – a false leg made out of an umbrella, a bicycle wheel on a harness, all sorts – but nothing's worked for her yet. Same is true for Colin."

Eric's attention turned to the toothless crocodile. "He needs some false teeth," he said.

"Yes, but I have yet to find any in crocodile size."

"At least he can't eat you."

"No, he's a teddy bear, really. Aren't you, Colin?"

With that, the crocodile turned over on to his back.

As he did so, his tail thrashed and knocked over Florence the flamingo once again.

DOOF!

"Colin loves tummy tickles!" said Sid. "Have a try!"

The boy did as he was told. To his delight, the crocodile actually seemed to laugh, by snapping his jaws together over and over.

SNAP! SNAP! SNAP!

"What did I tell you?" asked Sid. "Now, last but certainly not least, not in the bottom department, is Botty! Botty the baboon!"

"Botty must have the biggest bottom I have ever seen!" remarked the boy, as he studied the enormous rounded red thing at the top of the baboon's legs.

"All right! All right!" said Sid. "Don't go on about it. Botty is very sensitive about her botty! And it's not easy having just the one arm."

The baboon heaved herself up on to the man's shoulder as he fed her a crust of bread. As she did so, Botty's bottom poked right into Eric's face. Now, I don't know if you have ever had a baboon's bottom in your face, but, trust me, baboon's bottoms come very high on the *STINKOMETER.*

STINKOMETER

ROTTEN CABBAGE

DIRTY SOCKS

PIPE SMOKE

PONGY FEET

A DEAD RAT

UNWASHED UNDERPANTS

PIGEON POOP

DONKEY DUNG

A CAMPSITE TOILET

BABOON'S BOTTOM

Eric grabbed a wooden clothes peg from the table and put it on his nose.

"That's better!" he hummed in that strange voice you have when your nose is pinched.

"That's funny!" chuckled Sid, grabbing another peg and placing it on his nose. "Now I am sounding silly too."

Botty the baboon must have been intrigued too, because she grabbed a peg and put it on her nose!

"HONK! HONK!" she honked in a high-pitched honk, clearly delighting herself.

All three laughed.

"HA! HA! HA!"

"So," began the boy, "where did they all come from?"

"Oh! I, erm, 'borrowed' them all from the zoo."

"Borrowed?"

"Well, stole, really."

"Why?"

"All these animals have things 'wrong' with them. For me that is what makes them special. But no one thought they could survive so they were going to be 'put out of their misery'."

Eric's face turned pale.

"You don't mean...?"

"I do mean! Miss Gnarl would have been called in to give them a lethal injection!"

"Just like she's planning to do with Gertrude! We have to stop her, Uncle Sid!"

The old man looked at the clock on the wall. "It's already eleven o'clock. The zoo closes at five. We don't have much time!"

Just then there was a sound at the window.

TAP! TAP! TAP!

"Oh no!" hissed Eric, ducking his head.

"It must be the police!"

CHAPTER | 20 |

HIDE-AND-SEEK

"The police are after you?" whispered Sid.

"Yes!" replied Eric. "They wanted to evacuate me after Granny died, send me off to live with strangers, so I did a runner."

"No!"

"Yes. I have to hide," said the boy, scuttling across the room and opening a cupboard door. "Don't tell 'em I'm here!" he said as he found a place between the old pots and pans and shut himself in.

CLUNK!

TAP! TAP! TAP!

"Oh, for goodness' sake!" huffed Sid, making his way across the room to the door. "I know what three taps on the back window means and it isn't the police. It's—"

"Just your Bessie!" exclaimed a lady.

Eric spied through the crack in the cupboard door as a very jolly lady in a doctor's coat hurried into the room. She gave Sid the biggest bear hug, sweeping the poor man off his feet.

"OOF!"

All the animals swirled around her, hooting with delight.

"HONK! HONK! HONK!"

"SNAP! SNAP! SNAP!"

"Just your Bessie!" repeated Parker the parrot.

"Put me down, Bessie!" protested Sid with a shy smile that betrayed his true feelings for her. "Me tin legs might drop off!"

"Sounds like a perfect idea to me, my Sidney!" she chirped. Bessie had a joyful voice that made you instantly like her. You just knew she was someone who was full of **life** and **love** and **laughter.** "Then you won't be able to run away from me any more!"

"Put me down, Bessie! Please!" he repeated with a twinkle in his eye.

She did so.

CLANK!

"Spoilsport!" she huffed.

Over the man's shoulder she spied Eric peeping out of the cupboard. "My Sidney?"

"Yes?"

"Do you know you have a small boy hiding in your cupboard?"

"Yes, I do!" said Sid, scuttling over to the cupboard and opening the door. "This is my great-nephew, Eric! Come out of there, you!"

The boy pushed his way past the pots and pans and

climbed out of the cupboard.

CLUNK! Then he stood up, and put out his hand to shake, assuming that's what grown-ups did. The lady had other ideas. Just like she'd done to Sid, she scooped the boy off his feet and hugged him tight.

"Come to your Auntie Bessie!" she cooed.

Despite this lady being a perfect stranger, it felt nice to be hugged by her. She was all warm and soft and squishy, perfectly made for cuddles. It was almost as nice as being hugged by his mum or dad. Almost, but not quite.

"Put the boy down now, Bessie!" chuckled Sid.

"I don't mind at all!" exclaimed Eric.

Bessie twirled the boy around the room, trying her best not to trip over the animals, and set him down on the floor.

"Bessie is my neighbour—" began Sid. But no sooner had he begun speaking, than Bessie leaped in.

"I am my Sidney's neighbour! I live in the house right next door. Fortunately, the fence between our back gardens burned down in a bombing raid, so now I can come and go as I please. It couldn't be more perfect!"

Sid pulled a face. He wasn't so sure.

"Oh! You are naughty, but I like you!"

"Bessie comes over to—" began Sid again.

"I come over to feed the animals when my Sidney is out at work." A puzzled look crossed the lady's face, and she checked her little watch. "Talking of which, shouldn't you be at the zoo by now?"

"Yes and no," replied Sid.

"Yes and no? There is no yes *and* no. It's yes or no!" she teased.

"Yes, I should be there by now. But, no, I shouldn't, because I have been fired!"

"FIRED!" repeated the lady theatrically.

Sid nodded his head.

"FIRED?"

He nodded his head once more.

"FIRED? As in, fired fired?"

"YES! FIRED! AS IN FIRED!"

There was silence for a moment.

"FIRED?" she

asked again.

"YES!"

"But, my Sidney, you've been working at the zoo forever! You've devoted your life to that place! I know you've given blood, sweat, toil and tears! Why in the name of goodness would they fire you?"

Sid looked to Eric for help.

"Well, it's a long story," began the boy.

"Ooh, I like long stories!" said Bessie, sitting down at the kitchen table, and somehow stroking all the animals at once. "There, there, my darlings. I will feed you in a moment."

"We were worried about Gertrude," said Eric.

"The gorilla?" she asked.

"Yes, Gertrude the gorilla. The bombing raids had been frightening her like mad. And she broke out of her cage, and Batter—"

"Who?"

"The nightwatchman at the zoo," said Sid as the one-winged parrot hopped on to his shoulder.

"He was going to shoot Gertrude, and… well… we…"

"YES! GO ON! This is better than going to the pictures!" she cooed.

169

"Well, we had to wrestle the rifle from him, and he got knocked to the ground!"

"OOH, THE DRAMA!" she exclaimed.

"And we both got in big trouble."

"I shouldn't even have been at the zoo in the middle of the night," said Sid. "And certainly not with the boy. And now the zoo director general has decided that because Gertrude broke out of her cage the vet has to put her down."

"NO!" said Bessie.

"YES! He said she's a danger!" replied the boy. "But she's not. She's lovely! And I know because she's my best friend!"

"Oh dear," began Bessie. "Oh dear, oh dear. Oh dear, oh dear, oh dear…"

Eric looked to Sid. Was Bessie ever going to stop saying "oh dear"?

"Oh deary, deary me! So what are you going to do now?" she asked.

Eric replied, "Well, Bessie, it's simple!

We have to save her!"

CHAPTER | 21 |
CHARGE!

"How are we going to save Gertrude?" asked Sid. "Neither of us are allowed back at the zoo, and they are planning to put her down today as soon as it closes. That's just a few hours away now!"

"You will think of something, my Sidney and our Eric! I know it. And, while you do, I need to give these beauties their breakfast."

"BREAKFAST" must have been a trigger word for the animals, because instantly all seven sped as fast as they could towards her.

"OOOHHH!" trilled the lady as she saw them all coming.

Parker the parrot flapped her one wing, flying round and round in circles.

SQUAWK!

Sassy the seal swept out of her tin bath and landed with a slap on the kitchen floor.

HONK!

Ernie the elephant charged, his stumpy trunk swinging to and fro.

HOO!

Florence the flamingo hopped on top of Totter the tortoise's wicker shell, slowing them both down to a stop.

SCRAPE!

BOINK! BOINK! BOINK!

Colin the crocodile spun round, sweeping Florence off her foot.

SNAP!

DONK!

Botty the baboon leaped towards the lady with such gusto that she knocked her over like a skittle.

BASH!

Poor Bessie tumbled to the floor.

"WHOA!"

DOOSH!

Soon, all the creatures were crawling over her, and licking her face with their tongues.

"SLURP! SLURP! SLURP!"

"HELP!" she cried out.

"Come on now, my darlings!" ordered Sid, plucking them off one by one. "That's enough of that!"

Then he and Eric heaved the lady back to her feet.

"Why, thank you, kind sirs," cooed Bessie. She gathered herself together and announced, "I'll bring them their—"

"Don't say it!" urged Sid.

"B-R-E-A-K-F-A-S-T!" she spelled out. She knew the animals were smart but was pretty sure they couldn't spell.

Then she went back out of the door into the garden.

"So how are we going to rescue Gertrude?" asked Eric.

"I don't know, Eric. I really don't know. It seems impossible."

"Nothing is impossible!"

"Even if we do, where on earth are we going to keep her?" replied Sid, taking the weight off his tin legs by slumping down at the kitchen table.

"Here, of course!" exclaimed the boy.

"Oh my!" Sid's face turned a deathly shade of pale. "That's all I need now. A great big gorilla moving in!"

"She can sleep in my room!" said Eric.

"Oh yes! I forgot! You're moving in too! And, by the way, when you say your room, there isn't one! There's just one little bedroom at the top of the stairs."

"Well, I can sleep out there," reasoned the boy, pointing through the window to the little brick building at the end of the garden.

"That's the toilet!"

"Fine by me. If ever I need to go in the night, it couldn't be more convenient!"

"Eric, have you ever tried sleeping upright?"

The boy thought for a moment. It really was just

a moment because he was immediately sure that the answer was no. "I don't think so, no."

"Well, it's not comfortable!"

Then the boy's eyes widened with delight. "I've got it!" he exclaimed. "I've got it!"

"Got what?"

"An idea! I can sleep in here with Gertrude and all the other animals, and you can move in next door with Bessie!"

Now it was Sid's turn to blush as **red** as a very **red** thing. "Well, I don't know about that!"

"You like her, and she likes you."

"Well, let's not get too hasty…"

At that moment, they heard a chirp from next door: "BREAKFAST!"

Sid opened the back door. Immediately, all seven of his animal children scuttled out into the garden and next door to be fed.

"Please, Uncle Sid," pleaded the boy. "Help me rescue Gertrude."

"I want to! I love her too. But I just don't know how we can."

"If you won't help me, I'll do it on my own!"

"Not on your nelly!" exclaimed the old man. "I can't

let you sneak into the zoo alone after dark. Batter might shoot you!"

"So, you will help me?"

The old man sighed. "When there is danger and derring-do, Private Sidney Pratt reports for duty!" he said, saluting.

"YES!" exclaimed the boy.

"We'll find room for a gorilla. But Gertrude has to be the absolute last one. I really can't cope with any more animals. It's like Noah's ark in here!"

"Just Gertrude. I promise!"

"Good, good. Now, as with any military operation, we need to...

make a

plan!"

CHAPTER 22

THE PLAN

The pair didn't have long. It was now mid-morning, and even though Eric was supposed to be at school there was something infinitely more important to do than algebra.

Saving his best friend from certain death.

"Every secret military operation needs a code name," began the old soldier. "HUSH was one I remember from the First World War. What shall we call ours?"

Eric thought for a moment. "Bananas!"

"You what?"

"CODE NAME BANANAS!"

The old man wasn't convinced, but he didn't have a better idea. "Well, I suppose Gertrude does like bananas."

"And what we are trying to do is BANANAS!"

"You are right there! Let's get to work!"

First, Sid ordered the boy to fetch some paper and pencils from a drawer. Then the pair began sketching out a giant map of the zoo from memory. Together they could remember every pathway and animal enclosure. Next, they pinned the map to the wall. Now they had a view of all the exits and entrances, and, of course, the location of the gorilla's cage.

As the animals trotted back into the kitchen one by one, having been fed, Sid and Eric used the map to dream up a number of plans to rescue Gertrude, each one wilder than the last.

 THE PAIR DISGUISE THEMSELVES AS GORILLAS. Then they break into Gertrude's cage. There they stay until the zoo closes, when they reveal themselves to Gertrude and break out. This had one big flaw. Someone was bound to notice that there were three gorillas in the cage, and not one.

 THEY COMMANDEER A ROYAL NAVY WARSHIP from the Thames and sail up the canal that backs on to the zoo. Next, they blast a hole in the fence with a torpedo and snatch Gertrude. Then they make their escape through London's network of canals. This could be the perfect plan if not for one little thing: they didn't have a warship.

3

THEY DIG A TUNNEL all the way from Sid's back garden to Gertrude's cage. Then they could smuggle the gorilla down the tunnel to safety. But it was many miles from Sid's house to **LONDON ZOO**, and digging the tunnel would take a number of years. Sadly, they didn't have years to save Gertrude. Just a few hours.

4

THE PAIR PRETEND TO BE THE KING AND QUEEN on a royal visit to **LONDON ZOO**. Once inside, they say that they want to keep Gertrude as a souvenir of their visit. However, there was no chance these two could pass themselves off as royalty, however hard they tried.

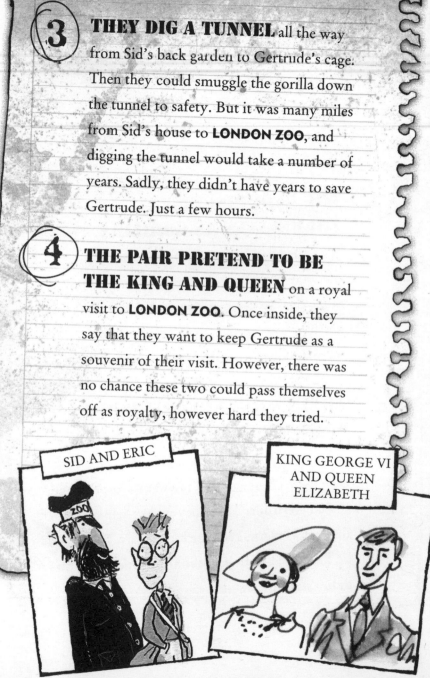

SID AND ERIC

KING GEORGE VI AND QUEEN ELIZABETH

5 **THEY BUILD THEMSELVES A GIANT PAPER PLANE** and launch themselves from the domed roof of St Paul's Cathedral, the tallest building in London. From there they swoop down over Gertrude's cage, and snatch her into the air. The problem was they'd used all the paper to draw a map of the zoo.

6 **THEY MAKE A DUMMY GORILLA** and smuggle it into the zoo. Once inside, when no one is looking, they swap the dummy gorilla with Gertrude, before making their escape. The big issue here was that they didn't have a dummy gorilla. With neither being good at arts and crafts, they also didn't have the faintest idea how to make one.

THEY SMUGGLE THEMSELVES INTO THE ZOO in sacks of food. Once

inside the zoo, they cut themselves out of the sacks, find Gertrude and make a run for it. The sticking point here is that they might very well find themselves being fed to a lion instead. Which, although nice for the lion, would not be so nice for them.

"ROAR!"

THEY BORROW UNIFORMS

from Bessie and pose as a pair of doctors. They rush into the zoo carrying a stretcher. If anyone stops them, they say they've been called to help a sick visitor, but instead smuggle Gertrude out on the stretcher under a sheet and bundle her into the back of an ambulance. One big problem: they didn't have an ambulance.

THEY MAKE THE WORLD'S TALLEST POLE VAULT by strapping a dozen or so walking sticks to one another. Then they pole-vault over the fence of the zoo and, once on the other side, break the gorilla out of her cage. This idea was dismissed as fast as it had been dreamed up. There was a very good chance the boy would break both his legs upon landing. This wasn't such an issue for Sid, what with his tin legs, but pole-vaulting at his age did not appeal at all.

 THEY STEAL A TANK, and smash through the fence to the zoo. Then they blast a hole in Gertrude's enclosure, scoop her up and speed out. If anyone tries to stop them, they could spin the big gun in their direction and **KABOOOM!** There was one teeny-weeny problem. This was very, very, very, very, very, very, very, very, very, very DANGEROUS!

What seemed like hours had passed, and the pair still didn't have a plan. It wasn't until Eric was idly staring out of the window that an idea finally hit him. Like most great ideas it was so BONKERS it was BRILLIANT!

"BINGO!" exclaimed Eric.

"BINGO! BONGO! What are you on about, boy?" asked Sid.

"I've got it!"

"Got what?"

"The plan!"

Sid clattered over to the window to see what the boy was staring at in the sky.

CLINK! CLANK! CLUNK!

"You don't mean we use a…?" began the old man.

"YES!

A barrage balloon!"

CLASSIFIED

PART THREE

NEVER SURRENDER

CHAPTER | 23 |

BALLOON

Eric had spotted a barrage balloon earlier when coming out of the underground station. It was one of hundreds flying over London. Barrage balloons might have looked like airships, but they were unmanned, and tethered to the ground. They had netting or cables stretching down from them to a military truck on the ground. They bobbed around in the skies over London to make it more difficult for enemy aircraft to enter the airspace. It meant the Nazi bombers and fighter planes had to fly high over the balloons to avoid them. This made them an easier target for the British anti-aircraft artillery (or big guns) on the ground. If the planes flew too low, then the guns couldn't spin round fast enough to hit them. Higher in the sky, the guns had much more chance of shooting them down.

"So talk me through this plan of yours," said Sid.

"We steal," began Eric, "I mean borrow a balloon, and fly it over the zoo. Once we reach the gorilla enclosure, we open the top of her cage and pluck Gertrude out. Then make our escape across the sky!"

The old man stared into space, lost in thought.

"Uncle Sid?" said the boy. "UNCLE SID! What do you think?"

"I think it's the least worst idea we've had!" he finally replied.

"That means it's the BEST!"

"Yes, I suppose it is!" said Sid, a flash of worry on his face. "But how do we know it's going to work?"

"We don't. Not until we try."

"Good answer! Now let's work out how we could fly a barrage balloon."

Upstairs in his bedroom, Sid had a collection of books about the First World War. In a book on old German war machinery, there was a chapter on Zeppelins. These were the airships used as bombers and scouts in the First World War. Unlike barrage balloons, Zeppelins had engines and a gondola underneath for a pilot. That's because they were designed to fly, rather than just float in one place.

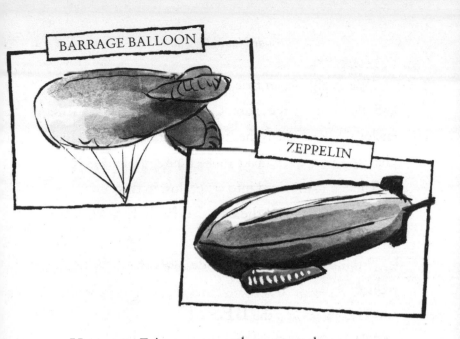

However, Eric was sure there must be some way of piloting a balloon, perhaps using the truck on the ground to which it was tethered. The problem was that time was running out. He looked at the clock on the kitchen wall. It was now one o'clock in the afternoon. There were only a few more hours until darkness fell. The zoo director general, Sir Frederick Frown, had said that Miss Gnarl was to put Gertrude down as soon as the zoo had been closed for the night, which was five o'clock. If the pair were going to save the poor gorilla from a lethal injection, they had to

act FAST!

CHAPTER | 24

DOWNED BOMBER

Leaving all the animals in the care of Bessie, Eric and Sid grabbed the map of the zoo from the wall and went off to find the base of the barrage balloon.

Keeping it in sight at all times, they travelled through the streets, round the back of gardens and along some wasteland. On a large common, a mile or so from Sid's house, squatted a military truck over which the big grey balloon was bobbing about in the sky. The balloon, shaped like a fat fish, was attached to the truck by a set of cables.

On closer inspection, the pair could see that the back of the truck was weighted down with bricks.

"BINGO!" said the boy.

"BINGO! BONGO! BUNGO! Whatever now?" demanded Sid.

"If we take enough bricks out, then…"

"The balloon will lift off, taking the truck with it!"

"Exactly!"

"But how are we going to steer it?"

"The truck's got a steering wheel!"

"I know that, silly! But that's to drive the truck, not the balloon flying through the air!"

"Mmm…"

This was a tricky one. If a Zeppelin used motors to fly from one place to another, then the barrage balloon needed one too. Not far from the balloon, Eric could see some children playing with something on the common. It was only when he stopped and stared that he realised what it was.

"LOOK!" he cried.

Sid squinted. "My eyes are not what they were."

"Come on!" said Eric, and he led the man by the hand towards it.

CLINK! CLANK! CLUNK!

A Luftwaffe bomber plane must have been shot down during the night and crash-landed on the common. The crew were nowhere to be seen. No doubt they had been hauled off for questioning by the police. Now, the giant plane had been taken over by some local teenagers, who were loving their new playground. They were climbing in and out and all over it, having the most marvellous time playing war games.

On seeing Sid approach, one snotty-nosed boy shouted, "Buzz off, you old codger! We're having fun!"

"Yeah, shove off, Grandpa!" added a spotty one.

"Sling your hook. And take that big-eared twerp with you!" mocked another.

"HA! HA! HA!" they all snorted together.

Sid said nothing. Instead he leaned on Eric's shoulder and yanked off one of his false legs.

CLUNK!

"I've got a good mind to boot you up the bottom!" shouted Sid.

"ARGH!" screamed the three terrified oiks, before fleeing across the common.

"Always works a treat!" said Sid, popping his leg back into place.

CLANK!

"I must remember to try that myself!" joked Eric. "Shame mine don't come off!"

"I have to remember not to take them both off at once, or it can backfire! Ha! Ha!"

"This is a beast!" said Eric, admiring the flying machine.

"It's a Junkers," observed Sid. "Designed only to bring death and destruction. I would like to shake the hand of whoever shot it down."

As Sid spoke, Eric paced around the craft. "There must be a part of it that we could use," he said.

"What do you mean?" asked Sid.

"I wish I had paid some attention in science class now, but there must be something we can take from this Junkers, which could help us fly that!" he said, pointing back to the truck with the barrage balloon floating above it.

"BONGO!" exclaimed the man.

"It's **BINGO!**" corrected the boy.

"BINGO! BONGO! BUNGO! BENGO AND **BANGO!** That's a clever idea!"

"Thank you!"

"Sadly, I didn't pay much attention at school either and everything I learned I forgot years ago. But you are right – there must be something we can use."

Our heroes went to work. They scoured the inside and outside of the bomber, trying to find anything that wasn't stuck down. There were some flying goggles and helmets, a propeller from one of the wings, three parachutes (unopened) and even a length of rope that might come in handy.

"What's in these?" asked the boy, pointing to some large cylinders.

Sid read the word printed on the metal out loud:

"*Sauerstoff?*"

"What does that mean?"

"It's something in German."

"I guessed that! But what?"

"Only one way to find out!" said Sid. With that, he turned the tap on. Gas **hissed** out fast, all but **blasting** the boy off his feet.

WHOOSH!

"Whoa! What is that?" asked Eric. He sniffed but couldn't smell anything. "Air?" he guessed.

"Oxygen!" exclaimed Sid. "Of course! For the crew if they had to fly high where the air is thin!"

"If it shoots out fast like that, maybe we can use it to power the truck along?" reasoned Eric.

"Maybe! Let's grab as many as we can carry!"

They hurried back across the common to the truck with their stolen treasure. At once they went to work, strapping the cylinders to the side of the truck and fixing the propeller to the front grille. The pair weren't sure whether the propeller was going to actually help the truck fly, but it looked **cool!**

The parachutes were packed in the back of the truck, in case of emergency.

As the sun hung low in the winter sky, they began the process of taking the bricks out of the back of the truck that were weighing it down. It was quite a task, as there were a few hundred or so bricks, and they had to take them out one by one. If they went too fast, there was every chance the truck could sail off into the sky without them, never to be seen again. After taking a good two hundred or so bricks out, Eric spotted one of the wheels of the truck lifting off the ground.

"Quick, Uncle Sid!
Jump in!"
he ordered.

The old man did as he was told and heaved himself up into the driving seat as fast as he could.

"I need you to act as a counterbalance!" called Eric from the back end of the truck.

Then, on his own, he took out brick after brick.

"The bonnet is lifting off the ground!" called Sid from the front. The whole truck had now been tipped up, and the bricks all slid out of the back at once.

CLONK! CLUNK!

With no bricks at all weighing it down,

the truck soared up into the air without Eric!

SWOOSH!

CHAPTER 25

JUMP!

"JUMP!" shouted Sid. But, as high as he could jump, Eric couldn't reach the truck, which was now floating away tied to the barrage balloon.

"I CAN'T REACH IT!" called Eric.

"AND I CAN'T CONTROL THIS THING!" hollered the old man.

Right now, the boy's only hope was a tall tree up ahead. The truck was floating straight towards it. If Eric could run fast enough, he might, just might, be able to scale the tree and leap on to the truck. He closed his eyes for a moment.

Gertrude, he thought. *What would Gertrude do?*

The boy had spent so many hours at the zoo watching the ape run and jump and climb.

So he began running towards the tree as fast as he could. Just like a gorilla, he launched himself high into the air.

WHOOSH!

Eric leaped at the tree.

He hit his head hard on the trunk…

DONK!

…and fell back down to the ground again.

THUD!

"ERIC!" shouted Sid from the truck, now sailing higher and higher into the air.

The boy found his glasses, picked himself up and climbed up the tree as if it were a ladder. When he'd reached as high as he could go…

WHOOMPH!

…he leaped off and landed on the bonnet of the truck.

DOINK!

"ERIC!" cried Sid from behind the steering wheel.

"UNCLE SID!"

It wasn't clear how shouting out each other's names could help matters, but they did so anyway.

As the truck began to tip dramatically forward with his weight, Eric began sliding down the bonnet. He desperately grasped on to the propeller they had attached to the front. They'd known it would be useful somehow! But the boy was slipping off.

"HELP!" he screamed.

"HOLD ON!" shouted Sid.

"The thought had occurred to me!" retorted Eric.

To make matters worse, the boy's dangling legs began whacking against the tops of the tallest trees on the common.

THWACK! THWUCK! THWACK!

"ARGH!"

With one hand holding on to the steering wheel of the truck, Sid pulled off one of his false legs…

POP!

…and leaned out of the window as far as he could go.

"GRAB HOLD OF MY FOOT!" he cried.

"You don't have any feet!"

"I have tin ones, remember!"

The boy's hands slipped down the propeller! He was holding on with just a finger and thumb. Any moment now, Eric was going to plummet to his **death.**

But just as he lost his grip…

"ARGH!"

…he managed to grasp the old man's battered tin foot!

CLUNK!

Eric held on to it as if his life depended on it. Which it did.

Using all his strength, Sid then hoisted the boy into the cab.

"Thanks, Uncle Sid," said Eric as he slumped on to the passenger seat, desperately trying to catch his breath.

He stared dead ahead through the windscreen. They were now heading straight for Battersea Power Station!

"UNCLE SID! LOOK OUT!"

The old man turned his head.

Together they cried,

"NOOOO!"

CHAPTER | 26 |

FOLLOW THE RIVER

"The air tanks!" shouted Eric.

Both he and Sid leaned out of the windows, pushed the cylinders downwards and unscrewed the nozzles.

wHOOSH!

Blasts of gas came out, propelling the truck higher into the sky. One of the back wheels just clipped the top of one of the tall chimneys.

DINK!

"Now, how do we get to the zoo from here?" asked Eric.

The old man looked down over London, a city he'd known his entire life. It suddenly looked unfamiliar from the air. Sid had never been in a plane before, but he had some sense of how to navigate from looking at maps during his all-too-brief adventure in the First World War.

"Let's follow the river until we reach Big Ben. Regent's Park is pretty much north from there. Once we find the park, the zoo is just at the top of it!"

"Righty-ho!" said Eric, rather settling into this role as co-pilot. The boy followed Sid's lead by putting on a leather flying helmet and goggles they'd taken from the downed Nazi bomber. Now, as they followed the snaking route of the Thames, they both felt like proper airmen. The pair smiled at each other.

"CODE NAME **BANANAS**

is underway!" declared Eric.

"It certainly is!"

After a while Eric became worried that they weren't moving fast enough. "What's the time?"

"Look!" replied the old man, pointing out of the side window of the truck. "You can see for yourself!"

Eric spotted the Houses of Parliament up the river. The tower known as Big Ben loomed over it, the face of its famous clock illuminated in the dark.

"Half past four!" said the boy. "We have to hurry. The zoo closes at five o'clock. So, we have just thirty minutes to save Gertrude!"

"Full speed ahead!"

The pair turned the valves on the air cylinders another cycle.

WHOOSH!

The truck picked up speed. Eric looked out of his window. The barrage balloon was still floating high above them. For now, they seemed to be passing over London undetected. The balloon floated silently in the dark sky above the city. However, if someone spotted them from the ground, they might assume it was an enemy aircraft.

The return of a dreaded Zeppelin, perhaps!

If the air-raid warning sounded, the sky would be a swarm of searchlights. There was every chance they could be shot out of the sky by anti-aircraft guns.

RAT! TAT! TAT!

Buckingham Palace was the next iconic building to loom into view, with its gardens on one side, and St James's Park on the other. Just ahead to the west was Hyde Park, with its famous lake, the Serpentine. As Sid and Eric flew over Marble Arch, they spotted Regent's Park with its gardens neatly laid out in a giant circle.

"LOOK!" said Sid, pointing.

"We're nearly at the zoo!" said Eric. "Let's hope we're not too late to save Gertrude!"

"Hold on, old girl! We're coming for you!"

From the air, they saw the last visitors leaving the zoo, and the gate being locked behind them. In the distance a clock chimed five times.

BONG! BONG! BONG! BONG! BONG!

"Five o'clock!" exclaimed the boy.

"We're moments away!" replied Sid.

Now they were sailing over the zoo itself. Using the cylinders strapped to the side of the truck once more and looking at the map they'd drawn of the zoo, they flew over the elephants, bears and camels. Up ahead was a giraffe, its tall neck stretched up into the sky.

"GIGI! DUCK!" shouted Sid, and they passed just over her head.

"There's a duck?" asked the boy.

"No. I was telling Gigi the giraffe to… Oh! Never mind!"

The boy looked at the map. "Giraffes are here, so Gertrude's cage should be just… THERE!" he exclaimed, pointing ahead.

"Well done. We'll make a soldier of you yet!"

"Let's begin our descent!"

Turning the air tank nozzles off, they began floating downwards, barely making a sound. Eric peered out of the window. To his horror, the gorilla was lying down flat on the ground of her enclosure. Standing over her in the gloom were three figures. From their outlines, it looked like Frown, Batter and Gnarl.

"NO!"

exclaimed the boy.

"It looks like we're too late!"

CHAPTER | 27 |

UNDER ATTACK

"Maybe not!" replied Sid. "First, they would have shot Gertrude with a dart to send her to sleep, before Gnarl gives her that lethal injection!"

Eric looked down out of the truck window. He spotted that Miss Gnarl had a needle in her hand. She was tapping the liquid in the tube, before leaning down to give the gorilla the poison.

Eric leaned out and shouted, "STOP!"

The three on the ground looked up. The sight of a truck dangling in the air from a balloon caused something of a shock. Immediately, Batter sprang into action.

"ENEMY AIRCRAFT OVERHEAD, SIR!" he shouted. "WE ARE UNDER ATTACK!"

Wasting no time at all, he hoisted his rifle into the air and fired.

BANG! BANG! BANG!

The bullets blasted straight through the truck, shattering the windscreen.

SHATTER!

"BATTER!" cursed Sid. "Let's go down, down, down!"

The pair angled the cylinders and twisted the nozzles open again.

WHOOSH!

The truck descended sharply.

BANG! BANG! BANG!

More rifle shots rang out, startling the whole zoo.

"HOO!" "SNORT!"

"SNARL!" "MURR!"

"WHOOP!"

The noise was like fireworks.

"I don't believe it!" spluttered Frown.

"It's Sidney Pwatt with that blasted boy!"

"GRRRR!" growled Gnarl.

"Let me shoot the gorilla, sir!"

"Go ahead, Batter!"

"GRRRR!"

Gnarl was not happy.

The man cocked his rifle.

CLICK!

"MORE AIR!"

said the boy.

He and Sid turned the cylinders to full blast.

WHOOSH!

The truck was now coming down sharply. It bashed the roof off the cage…

CLUNK!

…sending it falling.

"NOOOO!"

shouted Frown as the top of the cage clonked the three on their heads.

D O I N K !

DOINK! DOINK!

"OUCH!"

"OOF!"

"AWGH!"

They were all knocked to the ground.

DOOF! DOOF! DOOF!

Out cold.

The boy then opened his door and leaped out. Sid kept the truck floating a short distance from the ground. Eric stepped over Frown, Batter and Gnarl.

"Sorry about that, gentlemen and lady," he said, before he reached his friend.

Gertrude was lying on the ground motionless, her eyes closed.

"How is the old girl?" called Sid from the truck.

"Sleeping, I think… I don't know," replied Eric, before turning his attention to the gorilla.

"GERTRUDE! GERTRUDE! WAKE UP!"

he said, shaking her.

But there were no signs of life.

The boy sank to his knees and hugged the gorilla tight. "Oh, Gertrude, please wake up! We're here to rescue you!"

Eric held on to the big furry beast, rocking her gently. He felt something sharp poking out of her body. Just as Sid had predicted, it was a dart – the one to send to her to sleep, before she would be sent to sleep forever – and it was sticking out of her back. The boy wrapped his fingers round it and yanked it out.

PUTT!

The shock of the dart being pulled out must have woken Gertrude up, because immediately her eyes opened wide.

"GERTRUDE!" exclaimed Eric.

"HEE!" slurred the sleepy gorilla and pulled the boy close to her for a cuddle.

"You're alive!

You're alive!

YOU'RE ALIVE!"

"Cuddles are all well and good!" shouted Sid from the truck. "But this is a rescue mission!"

"I know! I know! I know!" called Eric. "But I just love her so much."

"Let's get her on board before these three wake up!"

"More cuddles later, Gertrude. I promise!" said Eric, before he wriggled out of her embrace, and scrambled to his feet. He leaned down, taking her huge hairy hand in his and tried to get her to stand up.

"HUH!" exclaimed the boy in effort, but the sleepy gorilla just wouldn't budge off the ground. Instead, she let out a giant yawn.

"YUH!"

"Uncle Sid!" called Eric. "I can't lift her!"

"Then tie this round her ankle!" said Sid, throwing down the rope they'd taken from the bomber.

Eric tied his best knot round Gertrude's ankle, who didn't seem the least bit bothered about it. Next, the boy clambered back into the truck, which was still floating at head height next to him.

With the extra weight of the gorilla, the truck needed big blasts of air from the cylinders to ascend.

WHOOSH!

"Where?"

"You'll see!"

Remembering his adventures from the night before, the boy reached out of the truck and angled his oxygen cylinder so they were powering along in the right direction.

They passed over the lions. One of them snapped at Gnarl's bottom with its razor-sharp teeth.

"ROAR!"

"GRRRRRRR!" howled Gnarl.

Dead ahead was the penguin pool.

Sid smiled. Now he understood what the boy meant. He too steered a course straight at it, at just the right height.

The dangling gorilla just missed the top of the overhanging tree, but Batter battered one of the branches.

"OUCH!"

The force of the impact made him lose his grip on the gorilla's arm.

"NOOOO!" yelled Batter, as he, Frown and Gnarl went plummeting through the air.

whOOSH!

"ARGH!"

"UWGH!"

"Grrrrrrrrrrrrrrrr!"

They landed in the penguin pool with three epic sploshes.

SPLOSH!

SPLOSH!! **SPLOSH!!!**

"SQUAWK! SQUAWK! SQUAWK!" squawked the penguins, clearly excited to have not one but three new playmates tonight.

Sid and Eric looked out and chuckled at the scene.

"HA! HA!"

"GET OFF ME!" Frown was screaming as he bobbed up and down in the water. "OR NO FISH FOR YOU TOMOWWOW!"

"MY RIFLE'S ALL WET!"

"**GRRRRRRRRRRRRRRR!**"

As the truck sailed on out of the zoo, Sid gulped. The seriousness of what had just happened was dawning on him.

"There's no going back now!" he uttered.

"I guess we're in deep **doo-doo,**" agreed the boy.

CHAPTER | 29 |
A HEFTY CATCH

Now Gertrude was having a whale of a time swinging from the rope. She'd woken up properly, and was propelling herself to and fro, so she could swing through the air.

"*WHEEE!*"

she was crying.

"Is Gertrude all right?" asked Sid, his face awash with worry.

Eric looked down out of the truck window. "I don't think I've ever seen her happier!"

"Ha! Ha! I hate to spoil her fun, but we'd better try to reel the old girl in!"

Using all their might, the pair heaved on the rope and opened the passenger-side door. Like fishermen reeling in a hefty catch, the gorilla eventually landed in the truck, right on top of Eric.

"OOF! She's heavy!"

Sitting in his lap, the gorilla put her arms round the boy, and gave him a big smacker on the cheek.

"*MWAH!*"

"Steady on, Gertrude!" protested Eric with a smile.

"You've just rescued the princess! It's her right to thank her knight in shining armour with a kiss. Now come on, old girl, slide over!"

Sid guided Gertrude to sit between them in the truck as Eric untied the rope from her ankle. Meanwhile, the gorilla had found a spare flying helmet and a pair of goggles. Not wanting to feel left out, she put them on. Now she looked like a proper pilot too.

Well, a great big, hairy one.

"WE DID IT!" exclaimed the boy.

"We really did!" agreed Sid.

Both hugged the gorilla, and the truck soared into the sky above Regent's Park.

"So how are you feeling, old girl?" asked Sid.

The gorilla stuck her tongue out and did the longest, noisiest raspberry.

"PFFFFFFFFFFFFFFFFFFFFFFFFFT!"

"She's never been better!" laughed Eric. **"Ha! Ha!"**

But that laughter was to be short-lived as suddenly the sounds of shells exploded all around them.

BOOM! BOOM! BOOM!

Anti-aircraft guns were firing at them from the ground.

"They must think we're a Nazi plane!" exclaimed Sid.

"NOOOO!"

cried the boy.

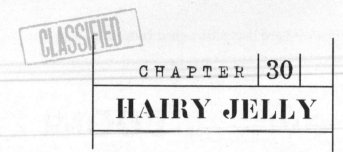
CHAPTER | 30 |

HAIRY JELLY

wooooOOOO!

wailed the air-raid warning.

BOOM! BOOM! BOOM!

Shells exploded all around them, rocking the truck as if it were on a roller coaster.

"WAAHAA!" screamed the gorilla in fear.

She began thrashing around in the cabin.

"GERTRUDE, NO!" shouted Eric, trying to calm her. But it was clear the shells were frightening her as much as they were frightening him.

"UP! UP! UP!" ordered Sid, and they piloted the truck higher and higher into the sky.

Still the shells exploded all around them.

BOOM! BOOM! BOOM!

Suddenly inside the truck the three felt a searing heat.

Sid looked out of the window at the barrage balloon

224

above. One of the shells must have exploded right next to it, because flames were now licking the side of the balloon.

WHOOF!

"What now?" asked the boy, his arms wrapped round Gertrude, who in turn had her arms wrapped round him.

"Any moment now that balloon is going to explode!"

"Oh no!"

"Oh yes. We have to make an emergency landing!"

Just then there was a mighty howl of engines over their heads.

ROAR!

Eric looked out of the truck.

The sky above them had been divided up like a jigsaw by hundreds of planes powering along in formation. There was a sea of swastikas on the tailfins. Sid, Eric and Gertrude had flown **SLAP BANG** right into the middle of one of the biggest bombing raids of the war so far.

"This can't be happening!" exclaimed Eric.

"It is!" snapped Sid.

The Nazi fighter planes began firing their guns to shoot the barrage balloon out of the sky to clear the way for the bombers.

RAT-TAT-TAT!

The three were now being attacked not just from below but from above too.

BANG! BANG! BANG!

RAT-TAT-TAT!

BOOM! BOOM! BOOM!

In no time, the balloon was hit!

It exploded!

KABOOM!

The scorching heat and blinding light of a massive fireball exploded into the sky. This was followed by the truck tumbling through the air.

WHOOSH!

"We're doomed!" shouted Sid, still clinging on to the steering wheel as they plummeted.

"**CODE NAME BANANAS** isn't over yet!" replied the boy. "We've still got the parachutes!"

Eric reached into the back of the truck for the three backpacks they'd taken from the downed Nazi bomber.

"Have you ever parachuted before?" asked Sid.

The boy shook his head. Then Gertrude shook hers too, perfectly reasonably. It is not every day you see a gorilla doing a parachute jump, now is it?

"Nor me," said the old man.

"But I've seen it at the Saturday morning pictures!" said the boy, fastening the backpack to Gertrude, before securing his own.

"You just have to pull this cord!" he said, pointing to a strap dangling from the pack.

As the ground below thundered into view, Eric opened the door to the cab. Air blasted in.

"We have to go now!" he implored.

Being a gorilla, Gertrude did not want to go. It seemed even more dangerous out there than it was in here.

She held on to the seat with her gigantic hands.

"GERTRUDE! GO! GO! GO!" shouted the boy.

But the creature just held on even tighter.

There was nothing for it! Eric would have to push her!

"I am sorry, Gertrude, but you give me no choice!"

With that, the boy shoved the gorilla out of the truck.

"WOO! WOO!" she whooped as she lost her grip and fell forward.

The gorilla hurtled towards the earth.

"The cord!" shouted the boy, just remembering. "She won't know how to pull the cord!"

229

With that, Eric leaped out of the truck head first,
flying through the air as fast as he could.
Above him, Sid leaped out and yanked his cord.

R-I-I-I-P-!

WHOOSH!

The parachute billowed
open, and he began floating
down to the ground.

Below him Eric could see
Gertrude with her arms stretched
out, flapping them like a bird.

FLUTTER!

FLUTTER!

FLUTTER!

Needless to say that wasn't going to help. If Eric didn't reach Gertrude soon, she would be nothing more than a splatter of **HAIRY JELLY** on the ground.

Keeping his arms tucked into his sides so he could fly through the air as quickly as possible, Eric fell faster than the gorilla.

WHOOSH!

In moments, he'd caught up with her.

Seeing her friend falling through the sky next to her, Gertrude grabbed on to him.

"WOO!" she exclaimed, a look of terror on her face. She held Eric so tightly that he couldn't move his arms.

"GERTRUDE!" he bellowed. "I need to pull your parachute cord!"

He looked down. If neither cord was pulled this instant, they were both jam, **HAIRY** or not. Just then he had an idea. The cord to open Gertrude's parachute was flapping in his face. Eric stretched out his neck and bit into it, before yanking his head back.

RIP!

WHOOSH!

The parachute opened and a huge smile spread across Gertrude's face.

"WHEE!" she cried as she floated gently downwards through the air.

Eric looked beneath him. The ground was heart-stoppingly close now.

In all the excitement, he had neglected to pull his own cord.

He did so…

YANK!

…but, DISASTER of DISASTERS, the cord came off in his hand.

RIP!

"NOoooOooooooooOOooooOooooOOOoooo!", yelled Eric.

Now, I know what you're thinking: Eric can't die now because we are only halfway through the book! There are loads and loads more pages! If he dies now, then there can't be any more story!

Well, you are, of course, RIGHT!

Eric doesn't die now.

He may have been tumbling through the sky without a parachute, but he is the hero of the book, so he is going to stay alive.

For now.

But how?

SPLASH!

Eric landed in the Serpentine. The huge lake in Hyde Park.

"OW!" shouted the boy as he hit the surface with a

THWACK!

It was as if his entire body
had been slapped all at once.
    Then he plunged deep into
the **black water.**

BLUB! BLUB! BLUB!
    The parachute on his back finally
opened, no doubt because of the impact.
Now, instead of saving his life, the parachute
looked as if it were going to end it. The weight
of the huge silk chute, all tangled up in the
water, was pulling him

down,
down,
down

into the **dark depths**
    of the lake.

Fighting for his life, Eric tore himself free from the parachute. Pushing his feet down against the bottom of the lake, he propelled himself up to the surface.

"AAAHHH!!!" gasped Eric. He had never been so grateful to take a breath in his life. He was **alive!**

But it was December – the water was absolutely FREEZING! If Eric didn't get out of the lake fast, then the cold would kill him. Unless, of course, the swans didn't peck him to death first.

"SQUAWK! SQUAWK!"

went the fearsome birds, attacking this intruder with their beaks.

"GET OFF!" he shouted, splashing them with water. The swans backed away and circled, buying the boy some time. Wiping water from his eyes, he spotted the truck hurtling towards him, trailing the flaming balloon in its wake.

WHOOSH!

If Eric didn't lunge out of the way, the truck was going to smash him to pieces.

The boy powered through the water as…

SPLASH!

…it crashed into the lake, missing him by an inch.

As the vehicle and the balloon sank, the boy looked up. An almighty battle was raging in the sky. Luftwaffe bombers were dropping their deadly loads all over London.

BOOM!
BOOM!
BOOM!

Nazi fighter planes were protecting them from British Spitfires, which were trying to shoot the bombers out of the sky.

RAT-TAT-TAT!

Meanwhile, shell after shell was being fired from the ground.

BANG! BANG! BANG!

Bombs hurtled to the earth as flaming planes twisted down like fireworks.

In amongst all this, Eric spotted two white circles in the sky.

Parachutes!

Gertrude and Sid were **alive!**

Eric swam towards the shore of the lake, splashing the swans and now a gang of ducks, which also seemed intent on attacking him…

"QUACK! QUACK! QUACK!"

…and he saw Gertrude land safely on the grass ahead.

"GERTRUDE!" he called out, though the gorilla didn't hear with the deafening noise of all the blasts.

The animal had clearly loved her flight, as she was leaping up and down on the spot, the parachute still flapping behind her. It was as if she were trying to propel herself back up into the air.

"WHOOP! WHOOP!" she whooped as she ran across the park, trying to fill the parachute with air again so she could lift herself off the ground.

Meanwhile, Sid landed, not so luckily, up a tall tree.

"OOF!" he moaned. "A branch is poking into my bottom!"

Eric heaved his soaking-wet and freezing body out of the lake, and rushed towards the tree.

"HELP!" cried Sid. "If I fall, I could break me legs!"

The boy paused at the bottom of the tree for a moment.

"I hate to be the one to have to tell you, but your legs are made of tin!"

"Oh yes!" remembered the old man.

"Still, they could get badly crumpled!"

"Can you climb down?" called up the boy.

"I would rather you climbed up," called down the man.

"Let me just help Gertrude!"

"Oh, now I get second place to an ape!"

"She might run off!"

"Yes, yes! You go and help Gertrude! Don't you mind about your poor old Uncle Sid!"

The boy sighed and shook his head, before racing off in the direction of the gorilla. She had attracted the attentions of the Serpentine's swans, who were circling her menacingly and hissing. *"HISS!"*

There was every chance that just as the swans had never seen a gorilla before, so the gorilla had never seen a swan before.

At first, Gertrude was her usual playful self, but when one of the swans pecked her bottom…

PECK! PECK! PECK!

…the gorilla was not amused. The mighty ape

turned round and snarled at the bird, baring her **fangs.**

"*HHHHIIIIISSSSS!*"

Instantly, the swans scattered.

"Gertrude!" exclaimed Eric, flinging his arms round her. "Thank goodness you're alive!"

The gorilla was clearly delighted to see him, as she planted another big slobbery kiss on his cheek.

"*MWAH!*"

"HA! HA!" the boy laughed, his face tickled by her fur. "All right! All right! I get it! You are pleased to see me, and I am pleased to see you! But we need to rescue Uncle Sid. Well, just Sid to you!"

Eric took the parachute pack off his friend. Then he led her by the hand over to the tree in which the old man was still stuck.

Bombs were exploding all over London, and Eric could feel his friend gripping his hand tighter with every

KABOOM!

"I've got you!" reassured the boy as the battle raged above them.

"Get a move on!" shouted Sid from the top of the tree.

"Hold your horses!" said Eric. "I'm coming to get you! Now wait here!" he said to Gertrude as he began shimmying up the tree.

Of course, Eric didn't speak gorilla, just as the gorilla didn't speak human.

Gertrude began shimmying up the tree too. Being an ape, she was awfully good at it, and made it to the top in no time. Despite not sharing a common language, the gorilla gestured to her back.

"What does she mean?" asked Sid.

"Hop on?" guessed the boy.

The old man did just that, and the pair were down on the ground in no time.

"Well, that was a first!" exclaimed Sid, still

on her back. "I have never travelled by gorilla before. I wonder if she'll carry me all the way home!"

At that, Gertrude shook her head and let the old man slide to the ground.

"No is the answer to that!" said Eric.

The boy took the gorilla by one hand, and Sid by the other.

"Did you go for another swim?" asked Sid, feeling that Eric's hand was wet.

"Sort of," replied the boy. "Now come on, please, let's get home. I am absolutely **f-f-freezing!**"

Seeing Eric shiver, the gorilla wrapped her huge, hairy arms round him to keep him warm.

"Thank you, Gertrude."

The ape just nodded and smiled, and together they began the long walk home. Eric was praying no one would stop them. How would they explain away a

great big gorilla?

CHAPTER 32

SUCKING ON A WASP

Bombs exploded all around the three as they dashed through the streets of London.

KABOOM!

Dust and debris were hurled into the air. The only light that illuminated their way home was the flickering red-yellow light of the fires from the bombs. Homes, shops, pubs were all ablaze, with firemen and local people fighting to put them out. Thick black smoke billowed into the sky.

London must have looked so strange to Gertrude, especially on a night like this. So, as much as the gorilla hugged Eric, he hugged her right back. They stayed close to the edges of the buildings, stalking in the shadows, keeping out of sight.

"Nearly there!" hissed Sid when they turned the corner into his road.

"STOP RIGHT THERE!" came a voice behind them.

The three froze in fear.

Eric turned round.

It was an air-raid warden, immediately recognisable by her round tin hat, which looked like an upside-down pudding bowl. The warden was not to be messed with. She had a sour face that made her look like she was sucking on a wasp. An official-looking badge on her chest read **NINA MISRA.**

"What are you three doing out on the streets after blackout? You must have heard the air-raid warning. You should be in a shelter. There's been no all-clear signal yet!"

The three said nothing, so she flicked on her torch to give them a closer inspection.

"A little boy, an old man and...

a gorilla!

What are you doing with a gorilla?"

Eric and Sid shared a look.

"Well?" demanded Nina.

"It's not a real gorilla, Mrs Misra," lied Eric, reading her name badge.

"Miss Misra!" she corrected. "Well, it looks like a real gorilla to me!"

"It's someone dressed up as a gorilla," said the boy. "We were coming from a fancy-dress party! I was going as a small, wet boy, and... er..."

"I was going as a zookeeper!" chipped in Sid.

The air-raid warden approached to get a closer look. She shone the light of her torch right at Gertrude's face, who squinted.

"It's an incredibly good gorilla outfit!" Nina remarked.

"She won't scrimp on gorilla outfits!" lied the boy. "Only the best will do!"

"Who won't scrimp exactly? Mmm? Tell me, who is under there?"

She put her face close up against the gorilla's and stared her in the eye.

"PFFFT!"

Gertrude blew a raspberry. Gorilla spittle flew all over the warden's face.

SPLURGE!

"She does that sometimes," remarked Eric. "My Aunt… um, erm, Bernard!"

"Bernard?" scoffed the warden. "Funny name for an aunt!"

"Bernard's a funny aunt!"

"Well, if you don't mind, Mrs… I mean, Miss Misra," began Sid, a hint of panic in his voice, "we should be getting home. My house is just over there, you see," he said, pointing. "And there are still Nazi bombers in the sky, so you can't be too careful."

With that, Sid led Gertrude and Eric across the road to his house.

"STOP RIGHT THERE!" came a bark behind them.

The three froze like statues in the middle of the road.

"Your Aunt Bernard walks exactly like a monkey too!"

"Technically, gorillas are not monkeys – they're apes," corrected Eric, unable to stop himself when it came to animal facts. "But, yes, she does like to get into character for fancy-dress parties! Goodbye!"

The warden marched over to the three of them. **"YOU'RE NOT GOING ANYWHERE UNTIL I SEE WHO IS UNDER THERE!"**

The lady put her hand on top of Gertrude's head, who by the look on her face didn't like it one bit.

"What are you doing?" asked Eric.

"I am going to pull her mask off!" said Nina, grabbing the tuft of hair on top of the gorilla's head.

"I wouldn't do that if I were you!" exclaimed Sid.

"Why not?"

"Aunt Bernard likes to stay in character the entire time!" explained the boy.

"What utter nonsense!" proclaimed Nina. With that, she yanked on the gorilla's hair.

"YEEE!" yelped Gertrude in pain.

"STOP!" pleaded Eric.

"The mask won't come off!" said the warden, pulling harder this time.

"YEEE!"

"PLEASE STOP!" Eric pleaded again.

"Or what?"

"YEEE!"

"Or Aunt Bernard might—"

But, before Eric could say whatever he was going to say next, the gorilla picked up the lady and raised her high above her head.

WHOOMPH!

"PUT ME DOWN!" protested the warden.

"PUT

ME

DOWN!"

CHAPTER | 33

TROUBLE

"Please, please, please put her down, Gertrude!" pleaded Eric.

The boy tried his best to reason with the gorilla. Despite being a gentle giant, Gertrude was still a giant when she wanted to be.

"Pretty please!" added Sid.

Gertrude tilted her head to one side, as if trying to understand.

"PUT ME DOWN!" ordered the lady.

"DOWN!" repeated the boy.

The gorilla nodded her head down, as if she were saying, "You want her to go down?"

"Yes!" said Eric, thinking he must be getting through. "DOWN!"

With that, Gertrude put the warden down head first into a dustbin.

Her helmet must have clunked against the bottom of the metal bin as she was knocked out.

"Oh no! Naughty Gertrude!" scolded the boy.

The gorilla shrugged and smirked. It looked very much like she'd done the whole thing on purpose.

"Is she all right?" asked Eric.

The pair heaved Nina out of the bin and laid her on the ground. Next, Sid leaned down and put his ear to the lady's mouth to listen. "She's still breathing, but she's out cold."

"We can't just leave her lying here on the road."

"No, of course not. Come on! Gertrude, that was very bad!" he said, wagging his finger at the ape.

Gertrude looked behind her, as if to say, "Who are you telling off?"

The gorilla sniffed dismissively.

"SNIFF!"

Peering at the reflection in a window of one of the houses, Gertrude flattened down the spiky hair on her head that had been so rudely tugged.

"Now, Eric, you grab the warden's arms and I will grab her legs! On three! One, two, three!"

The pair picked Nina up, and gently sat her on the bench of a nearby bus stop.

"Miss Misra can sleep it off there!" remarked Sid.

"And, of course, it's handy if she needs to catch the bus home in the morning!"

"Exactly!" concluded the old man, before turning

his attentions to the gorilla, who was still preening herself like a posh lady in a make-up shop. "Now come along, trouble."

He and Eric took Gertrude by the hands and led her down the deserted road to his home. As they did so, the all-clear signal sounded.

woooHOOO!

To their great relief, the night's bombing raid was over. Those Luftwaffe bombers that hadn't been shot out of the sky were now flying back to Germany.

CHAPTER | 34 |

PINK FRILLY NIGHTDRESS

When Sid and Eric walked through the door of the old man's little terraced house, it wasn't clear who was more pleased to see them.

The animals or Bessie!

Sid's number-one fan had been waiting up in her pink frilly nightdress all night for their return.

"MY SIDNEY!" she exclaimed, powering down the corridor, heading straight for him.

The lady bustled past the animals and launched herself at her love. His eyes were opened wide in shock as she wrapped herself round him. "THANK THE GOOD LORD YOU ARE SAFE!"

254

"I was," he said, struggling to breathe as she was holding him so tight. Such was the force of her jump that Sid's tin legs couldn't take it.

CRANKLE!

They rocked backwards and the pair tumbled to the floor.

DOOF!

Bessie ended up sitting on top of Sidney, who was spread out on the floorboards.

"OOH, SIDNEY! YOU OLD DEVIL!"

Eric chuckled to himself. "Ha! Ha!"

"Can someone please help me up?" demanded Sid.

"Let's not be too hasty!" hooted Bessie.

"No, let's be very hasty! Chop! Chop!"

Eric helped Bessie to her feet first.

"I enjoyed that!" she sighed.

Then they both helped the old man to his tin feet.

"I didn't! I could hardly breathe!" spluttered Sid.

Next, he greeted his animal children. They were all so pleased to see him. It is quite something being pawed at, nuzzled and licked by a parrot, a baby elephant, a seal, a flamingo, a crocodile, an enormously bottomed baboon and, bringing up the rear, a giant tortoise, all at once.

"I've missed you, my beauties!" said Sid.

"And I know who this is!" cooed Bessie on seeing the gorilla. "Ooh, she's glorious!"

"The newest member of our family!" announced the boy. "Meet Gertrude!"

The gorilla began greeting all the other animals as if they were old friends. Some she might have remembered from the zoo, others she was meeting for the first time. No matter, she showered them all with love, with cuddles, strokes and kisses galore.

"Who would ever want to hurt this **magnificent** lady?" exclaimed Bessie. "Now, what does Gertrude like to eat? I could cook her up a nice welcoming treat!"

"Bananas are her favourite!"

"No bananas, I'm afraid! There is a war on!"

"Raisins?"

"I just baked a fruit-and-nut cake! That has a ton of raisins in it!"

"Yummy! I'm sure she'd love that!" exclaimed the boy.

Eagerly, Gertrude nodded her head and licked her lips.

"SLURP!"

"And I would too!" said Sid. "Oh, and a nice cup of cocoa!"

"Oh well, if you are doing cocoa and cake, I would love some too, please! I'm starving!" added the boy.

"Let me get cracking!" said Bessie as she bustled out of the back door.

The boy slumped down on a chair in the kitchen and yawned.

"I'll have my cocoa and cake, and go straight to bed," said Eric.

The old man's eyes flashed with fear.

"What?" asked the boy.

"We can't stay here!" said Sid.

"Why not?"

"They'll be on to us."

"Who?"

"Everyone! Frown, Batter, Gnarl! They might have already called the coppers. And then there's the air-raid warden out there! She'll wake up soon and she knows exactly where I live."

"How come?"

"I pointed at the house."

"Oh yes. That wasn't too clever!"

"Wasn't too clever!" repeated Parker the one-winged parrot, who was perched on Eric's shoulder.

"Shush, you!" said Sid.

"Shush, you!" the parrot repeated.

"Cheeky little so-and-so, isn't she?" chuckled Sid.

"Where can we go?" asked the boy.

"We need to get out of London! A fully grown gorilla is far too big for this little house anyway. No offence, Gertrude!"

The gorilla, who was busy pulling **fleas** out of Botty the baboon's fur and eating them, looked back at him and shrugged.

"We need somewhere with open spaces so she can lollop around to her heart's content!"

Eric had **never** been out of the city in his short life. Some of the other children at his school bragged about day trips to the seaside, and Eric had always wanted to go. It was something his mum and dad had often talked about, but, alas, it was not to be.

"How about we take Gertrude to the seaside?" suggested Eric.

"In December?" spluttered the old man. "It'll be blowing a gale!"

"Oh no. You're right. It's a stupid idea!" he replied, downcast.

Suddenly Sid's face brightened. "It's not a stupid idea! It's a **brilliant idea!** No one else will be visiting the seaside at this time of year. We'll have the place to ourselves! There's an old guesthouse I used to stay at way back when I was a boy. In the last century it was! Oh, I loved it. It was just outside Bognor Regis, up on a hill, and from there I could see all the British warships going to and from Portsmouth Harbour. I went back there just before war broke out to take a trip down memory lane, but it was all boarded up. It would be the perfect place for us to hide out!"

"Brilliant! What's it called?" asked the boy.

"Seaview Towers!" said Sid.

"Seaview Towers!" repeated Parker the parrot.

"Seaview Towers!

Seaview Towers!"

CHAPTER | 35 |

FRUIT-AND-NUT CAKE

So, over cocoa and fruit-and-nut cake (which was mostly wolfed down by the animals), Sid and Eric started to put together the latest part of their mission, **CODE NAME BANANAS**. It was now nearly midnight, and the police could come knocking at any moment. It was decided that they should depart at dawn for the seaside with Gertrude, leaving the parrot, the baby elephant, the seal, the flamingo, the crocodile, the giant tortoise and, of course, the enormously bottomed baboon to stay with Bessie next door.

The problem was how were Sid and Eric going to get Gertrude to the seaside? From London, Bognor Regis was a good fifty miles or so away. Sid didn't own a car. Neither did Bessie. Nor, of course, did Eric. Or Gertrude, for that matter. Gorillas just can't get the insurance.

It was far too far to walk, especially if you had old tin legs like Sid. So a train seemed like the best option. But how could they smuggle a gorilla on to a train without everyone noticing?

In the corner of the kitchen, Eric spotted a battered old wheelchair.

"Maybe we can use that?" he exclaimed.

"For me?" asked Sid.

"No, for Gertrude!"

"The hospital gave that wheelchair to me after the war. The nurses said I should use it if I ever needed to take the weight off these tin legs of mine!"

"We could push Gertrude in it!"

"But everyone would still be able to see she is a gorilla!"

"Then we need to disguise her!"

"As what? An **orang-utan?**"

"NO!" said Eric. "That would be plain silly."

"Nobody will be looking for an escaped orang-utan," reasoned Sid. "All we'd need to do is smother her in marmalade! Then she'd be all orange!"

Gertrude pulled a sour face. She didn't like that idea one bit!

"NOOO!" exclaimed Eric.

"All right, all right, there's no need to shout."

"No need to shout!" repeated Parker the parrot.

"We need to disguise Gertrude as a person!" stated Eric.

They both turned to look at the gorilla, who was sitting cross-legged on the floor, demolishing the fruit-and-nut cake Bessie had brought round.

CHOMP! CHOMP! CHOMP!

Gertrude then rose to her feet and pattered around the room on all fours, scratching her bottom as she hunted for crumbs.

"How on earth are we going to do that?" asked Sid.

"We need to dress her up!"

"We can dress her up as much as we like! But what about that face of hers? Beautiful though it is, it's a bit of a giveaway! It's very gorilla-ish!"

"You're right," mused the boy. "Maybe she could wear a gas mask?"

"I don't think she's going to like that!"

"It's worth a try!"

Everyone in Britain had been issued with a gas mask because of the fear of a poison-gas attack by the Nazis.

So Eric picked up Sid's from the kitchen table and tried to fit it over Gertrude's face.

Unsurprisingly, the gorilla yelped: "EEEEHHH!" and immediately yanked off the mask and hurled it across the room. Luckily, Parker the parrot ducked just in time.

"SQUAWK!"

The gas mask hit a framed photograph on the wall.

SMASH!
CLUNK!

The boy winced. "Not my best idea!" he admitted.

The gorilla nodded her head in agreement.

Eric went over to pick up the photograph. It was an old faded black-and-white image of a much younger Sid on his wedding day. He was standing proudly next to his bride, Aunt Hilda, who was wearing a veil.

Sid's wife, Hilda, had become ill and died many years before, but he had many remembrances of her all over the house.

"How about we put Gertrude in a wedding dress?" exclaimed the boy.

Sid spat out his cocoa.

SPLURT!

It sprayed all over Botty the baboon, who scurried up the net curtains.

"A wedding dress?" thundered Sid. "Why would we put Gertrude in a wedding dress?"

"Then she could have a veil like Aunt Hilda's to cover her face!"

The old man fell silent for a moment. "That's not a bad idea!"

"Thank you!" replied the boy proudly.

"But where are we going to get a wedding dress from at this late hour?"

"Might Bessie have one?"

"I doubt it. Bessie has never been married."

"Not yet!" teased the boy cheekily.

"Steady on!"

"Maybe she could help us make one!"

"Out of what?"

The boy stood up, stepped over the crocodile and made his way to the window. There he took hold of the net curtain and wrapped it around himself. "Out of this!" It was long and white and crumply, not unlike a wedding dress.

"Clever boy!" chirped Sid.

"Clever boy! Clever boy!" repeated Parker the parrot.

The baboon leaped down off the curtain rail and squatted on the boy's head.

"Not now, Botty!" said Eric, lifting her off and placing her on the table.

Just then, Bessie bustled through the back door, carrying a tray piled high with biscuits.

"Here you are, my loves!" she cooed, and

immediately all the animals surged towards her, eager to be fed. "Ooh! Steady! One at a time!" she exclaimed.

"Bessie," began Sid, "we need you to help with something, please."

"Anything for you, my Sidney! You know that!"

"I need you to help make a wedding dress!"

Tears welled in the woman's eyes. "Oh, my very own Sidney! I never thought the day would come!"

She rushed over and embraced him, planting kisses all over his face.

"MWAH! MWAH! MWAH! I do! I do! I do! I will marry you, my Sidney! We can be together for all eternity, and beyond!"

Sid gulped.

"GULP!"

As politely as he could, Sid unhooked Bessie from him.

"No, no!" he spluttered. "The wedding dress is not for you!"

"Oh! So, you have another woman! Would you care to tell me the name of this floozy?" she demanded.

"It's Gertrude!"

The lady looked mightily confused, and more than a little disgusted.

"You are going to marry a monkey?"

"Gorillas are apes!" corrected an irritated Eric.

"You are going to marry an ape?"

"No!" snapped Sid. "No one is marrying anyone. We are going to disguise Gertrude as a bride."

"Whatever for?"

"So she can have a veil covering her face!" said Eric. "Then no one will know she's a gorilla!"

"Well, that is clever! Very clever indeed. Of course I will help. Let's get to work!"

That's exactly what they did. They tore down the net curtains, measured Gertrude and set about making her the prettiest wedding dress they could.

CHAPTER | 36 |

BOY BRIDESMAID

As the sun began to rise over a smouldering London, the bridal outfit was finally complete. It comprised:

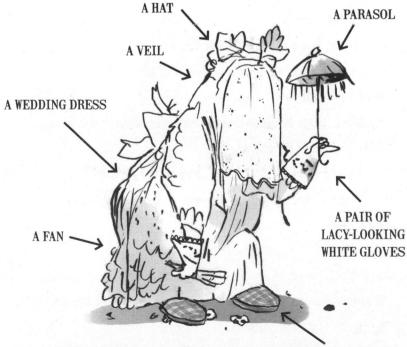

A HAT

A PARASOL

A VEIL

A WEDDING DRESS

A PAIR OF
LACY-LOOKING
WHITE GLOVES

A FAN

SID'S SLIPPERS (THESE WERE THE ONLY SHOES THAT FITTED
GERTRUDE'S GINORMOUS FEET AT A HUGE STRETCH)

They could only bribe Gertrude to be dressed in all this with one thing. More fruit-and-nut cake.

MUNCH! MUNCH! MUNCH!

As the gorilla demolished another of Bessie's delicious home-made treats, the three could fuss around her, getting her ready for the train trip to the seaside.

"She's never looked lovelier!" cooed Sid.

"What a beautiful bride!" agreed Eric.

"I always cry at weddings!" blubbed Bessie.

"It's not an actual wedding!" said Sid.

"Oh yes."

"It's just a disguise," added Eric.

"And a ruddy good one at that!" admired Sid. "Now sit down, old girl!"

With that, he gently sat the cake-munching gorilla down in the wheelchair.

MUNCH! MUNCH! MUNCH!

"Now, Uncle Sid, you have to dress like the groom!" said Eric.

"Me?"

"Yes! You can pretend you two just got married and if anyone stops you and asks, you just say you are going to the seaside for your honeymoon!"

"But… but… but…" protested Sid.

"No buts, Sidney!" said Bessie sternly. "Listen to the boy. He's a good deal smarter than you! Go upstairs and put your best suit on!"

"Harrumph!" harrumphed the man. "What about the boy?"

"Oh yes!" agreed Bessie. He'll need a cover too!"

Eric shifted uncomfortably on his feet.

"I know!" exclaimed the lady. "You can be a pretty little page boy!"

"What's a page boy?" asked Eric.

"It's like a boy bridesmaid!"

"No, thank you!" he snapped.

"Now come on, everyone is getting into character. You need to too!"

"Well, what do page boys wear?"

"Normally, Victorian sailor suits!"

"NO!" shouted Eric.

"Let me see what I can rustle up! I'll be back in a jiffy!"

Eric barely had time to sulk before Bessie popped back to her house next door and returned with a ragbag of what looked like her own undergarments.

"I am not wearing any of that!" huffed the boy.

"Wait! Let me work my *magic!*"

In moments, she had adorned him in various frilly lace bits and bobs. He looked like some sort of silly little toff from the olden days.

"I am not wearing this!" he grumbled again.

"There's no time to argue!" said Bessie.

Just then there was a thunderous banging on the door.

KNOCK! KNOCK! KNOCK!

"Oh no!" hissed Eric.

Sid was still upstairs getting changed into his wedding suit.

"Shall I open it?" asked the boy.

"No, no," replied Bessie. "Let's just stay silent and maybe whoever it is will just go away!"

KNOCK! KNOCK! KNOCK!

It was louder this time.

"Don't say a word!" whispered Bessie.

"DON'T SAY A WORD!" repeated Parker the parrot.

"Shut up, you stupid bird!" hissed Bessie.

"SHUT UP, YOU STUPID BIRD!" repeated the stupid bird.

KNOCK! KNOCK! KNOCK!

"WE CAN HEAR YOU IN THERE!" called a voice through the letterbox. It sounded an awful lot like Miss Nina Misra. "OPEN THIS DOOR AT ONCE OR WE WILL BE FORCED TO BREAK IT DOWN!"

"BREAK IT DOWN! BREAK IT DOWN!" repeated Parker.

"ALL RIGHT, THEN! WE WILL!" replied Nina.

"HIDE!" hissed Bessie. "Don't worry! I'm coming! I'm coming!"

She shut the kitchen door behind her. Eric knelt down at it so he could spy through the keyhole. From there, he could see Bessie answer the door to the air-raid warden. This time she was not alone. Nina was flanked by two policemen. All had grave expressions on their faces.

"Yes? Can I help you?" asked Bessie as innocently as she possibly could, which was not that innocently. She was too nice to be good at lying.

The warden looked confused to see this lady answer the door.

"Is there an old man, a young boy, and a, er, lady dressed as a gorilla who live here?" demanded Nina.

"Let me think!" replied Bessie. "No! Just me! I live here all alone. No husband. No son. And definitely nobody dressed as a gorilla. I am sure I would remember that. I'm sorry, but you must have the wrong house! Goodnight!"

The lady went to close the door, but the warden put her boot in the way.

"Not so fast!" said Nina. "We heard another voice through the letterbox. A squawky-sounding voice. Who was that?"

"I don't know what you are talking about!" lied Bessie. "Now I really must get to bed."

"GET TO BED! GET TO BED!" repeated Parker.

"There it is!" exclaimed Nina.

"It's just an echo!" lied Bessie.

"An echo?"

"AN ECHO! AN ECHO!" repeated the parrot.

"See!" exclaimed Bessie. "There it goes again! Now I really am very tired, so please let's call it a night. If I do see an old man, a young boy and, of course, anyone dressed up as a gorilla, you will be the first to know!"

Bessie tried to close the front door again, but the warden put her heavy hand up against it. "You don't mind if we have a quick look around the house, do you?" she asked.

Bessie could protest no more. The warden, flanked by the two policemen, marched into the hallway.

"We will start in there!" said the warden, pointing to the kitchen door.

Hiding behind the door on his knees, the boy gulped.

They were all done for!

CHAPTER | 37 |

RUGBY TACKLE

Eric put his shoulder up against the kitchen door to stop it from opening. But his boyish frame was no match for Nina and the two burly policemen with her. They began shoving the door open as Bessie was begging for them to stop.

"NOOOO! PLEASE! YOU'LL FRIGHTEN THE ANIMALS!"

"ANIMALS? WHAT ANIMALS?" demanded Nina.

"Oh, just a pair of tadpoles, but they are very sensitive to loud noise!"

Just then Eric could hear Sid clunking down the stairs on his tin legs.

CLINK! CLANK! CLUNK!

"You can't go in there!" he cried.

"Oh, it's you!" replied Nina. "So you were lying, lady! This man does live here. Now we are going to arrest that person in the gorilla costume. Or, from the pungent stink coming from the kitchen, I'm beginning to think it might be an actual gorilla! In which case we will arrest it!"

The kitchen door burst open.

DOINK!

The air-raid warden and the two policemen were met by the most unexpected sight.

It was a wildlife park! A little wildlife park, but a wildlife park, nonetheless.

All the animals reacted to these three uninvited guests in different ways…

Parker the one-winged parrot leaped on to the back of a chair.

Ernie the elephant raised his stumpy trunk and waved with it as if to say "hello".

Sassy the sightless seal honked.

"HONK!"

Totter the giant tortoise with no shell stopped in his tracks.

Florence the one-legged flamingo was so shocked she *toppled* right over.

DONK!

Colin the toothless crocodile scuttled under the table in fear.

SCRAMP!

Botty the one-armed and big-bottomed baboon scratched her big bottom with her one arm.

SCRITCH!

And last, but certainly not least, Gertrude the gorilla took a break from licking the cake plate clean and lifted up her bridal veil. Then she blew the longest, loudest raspberry you have ever heard in your life.

"PFFFFFFFFFFFFFFFFFFFFFFFFFFFFFFFFFT!"

The raspberry went on for so long that it shocked everyone who heard it into the deepest silence. When she'd finally finished, Eric remarked, "I think that meant 'hello'!"

The three intruders looked absolutely appalled.

"You aren't allowed to have all these exotic animals in your house!" said the first policeman. "I am putting you all **under arrest!**"

"Even the animals?" asked the other.

"Yes! Even the animals!"

"On what charge?"

"We'll think of something!"

As the policemen unhooked their handcuffs from their belts, Sid sprang into action.

"There's only one thing for it! DINNER TIME!"

This cry made all the animals charge towards Sid.

WHOOSH!

They knocked the air-raid warden and the two policemen to the floor...

BASH!

BISH!

BOSH!

...trampling all over them in a rush to be fed.

TRAMPLE! **TRUMPLE!** **TROMPLE!**

"ARGH!"
"GET OFF!"

"I'VE GOT A GREAT BIG BABOON'S BOTTOM IN MY FACE! " they cried.

With the three pinned to the ground, it was the perfect moment for the other three to make their escape. Eric raced round the back of Gertrude's wheelchair and

Zipped

out of the back door.

"Come on, Uncle Sid!" he cried.

They trundled out of the garden, across the burnt-down fence, through Bessie's house, Gertrude swiping a cake tin on the way, and out of her front door. The air-raid warden must have managed to scramble to her feet, as she gave chase down the road.

"STOP RIGHT THERE!" shouted Nina.

Bessie emerged and ran after the air-raid warden.

"NO! YOU STOP RIGHT THERE!" she shouted.

Taking a running jump, Bessie performed an expert rugby tackle.

THUMP!

Nina fell to the ground…

THUD!

…Bessie on top of her.

"OOF!"

"GO, MY SIDNEY, GO!" shouted Bessie as she pinned Nina to the road.

"Thank you, my dear!" called back the old man, now in the distance. "This way!" he hissed to Eric. Together they pushed Gertrude in the wheelchair along a maze of back alleys so they couldn't be followed.

The three had to speed all the way to the station if they were going to escape to the seaside. They trundled along the empty roads as fast as they could. The gorilla didn't seem to mind the lumps and bumps of the rubble on the ground too much. She was too busy munching on another fruit-and-nut cake from Bessie's house to worry.

MUNCH! MUNCH! MUNCH!

As they neared the railway station, the streets began to hum with passers-by. Needless to say, this wild wedding party received some strange looks. Eric and Sid thought it best to brazen it out by greeting people cheerily.

"HELLO!"

"GOOD MORNING!"

"SUPER DAY FOR IT!"

Eventually the three reached the station. Now was the real test. Could they really board a train with a

great big gorilla?

CHAPTER 38

THE TASTE OF CARDBOARD

CLASSIFIED

Victoria station was one of the largest in London. It was a huge, ornate building, almost like a cathedral, but bustling with people and humming with noise. Most passengers were arriving into London rather than departing at this time of the morning, so the ticket queue wasn't too long. After buying two adult and one child single tickets to Bognor Regis (sadly there weren't any discounts for gorillas), they trundled on to the station concourse. This was where the **ARRIVALS** and **DEPARTURES** boards were. They scoured them, searching for the first train to Bognor Regis.

"Bognor Regis train! Platform eighteen!" exclaimed Eric, his eyesight much better than Sid's. "Ten past six. That gives us five minutes!"

"It's right at the other end of the station. No time to

dilly-dally. Lct's go!" said Sid.

Making sure Gertrude's veil was still hiding her face, Eric pushed her in the wheelchair along the concourse.

When they passed a bin, the boy reached in and took out a handful of different-coloured train tickets. Trailing behind the happy couple, he ripped them up into little pieces and threw them over the pair to complete the appearance that they were newly married.

"CONFETTI!" he cried.

"Clever boy!" remarked Sid.

The boy glowed with pride.

As they hurried towards platform eighteen, they passed some newspaper sellers standing at stalls, plying their trade.

To Eric and Sid's horror (not Gertrude's as gorillas can't read*), they were shocked to see the morning's newspaper headlines. They were all on display in posters on the front of the sellers' stalls. As if that wasn't enough, the men in cloth caps and brown overalls were calling out the headlines to drum up sales.

---

* Which is a great shame because I would very much like gorillas to buy my books.

"How many times do I need to say that a gorilla is **not** a monkey – it is an ape!" hissed Eric as they passed the stalls.

"**Shush!**" shushed Sid. "Now is not the time!"

As was usual during wartime, there were plenty of policemen on duty at London railway stations looking for anything or, rather, **anyone** suspicious.

A Nazi spy perhaps?

An escaped prisoner of war?

A downed Luftwaffe bomber pilot trying to smuggle himself back to Germany?

So this weird wedding party aroused suspicion. They certainly made an unusual sight.

The way Sid's tin legs clanked as he walked.

CLINK! CLANK! CLUNK!

The rusty old wheelchair carrying the bride, who was completely covered from head to toe in what looked like some old net curtains.

And, last but not least, a small boy dressed in what looked like a pair of lady's bloomers. Either he was some kind of time-traveller, or had got dressed in the dark, or just liked wearing lady's bloomers. Whichever it was, it made the policemen stop and stare.

"Just carry on walking!" hissed Sid. "Don't look round!"

Eric felt as if there were a hundred pairs of eyes staring at him and he began to go as red as a bottle of tomato ketchup.

"Tickets for Bognor Regis, please!" barked the ticket inspector at the entrance to platform eighteen.

"Yes! Yes!" chirped Sid. His hands were shaking so much that he dropped the tickets on the ground.

"Silly me!"

When he bent down to pick them up, his head clonked with Gertrude's.

"URGH!" she moaned from under her veil.

The ticket inspector was alarmed at the noise. "Is your wife all right under there?"

"Yes!" replied Sid. "She just has mixed feelings about the marriage."

The inspector shook his head. "Sounds like it. Third class is the front four coaches!"

"Thank you kindly!"

Just as the trio were about to hurry off to board their steam train to the seaside, they felt a tap on their shoulders.

"Excuse me. May we have a word?"

Sid and Eric turned round. Two tall policemen, made even taller by their tall helmets, loomed behind them.

"Can we see your papers, please?" asked one.

Eric and Sid fumbled in their pockets for their **IDENTITY CARDS.** In wartime, these might need to be produced at any moment.

The policemen studied the cards, before handing them back.

"Well, thank you, we'll be on our way!" said Sid.

"STOP!" ordered one of the policemen. "What about the lady's?"

Sid and Eric looked at each other. How were they going to get out of this particular pickle?

Gertrude didn't have an **IDENTITY CARD.** Gorillas didn't have **IDENTITY CARDS.** That's because they were gorillas.

TOOT! TOOT! went the engine, signalling that the train was ready to depart.

"I'm very sorry, officer, but we're going to miss our train!" said Eric.

"That is not my concern. The safety of this great nation is at stake! I need to see the lady's **IDENTITY CARD.** NOW! Hand it over, miss!"

Gertrude was not enjoying the hold-up. Her gloved hand reached up from under her dress and yanked on the policeman's nose.

"OW!"

Sid slapped her hand away.

"Sorry. Just her little joke! And she's a Mrs! We just got married," corrected Sid.

"Congratulations are in order, then," replied the policeman rubbing his nose. "But we need to see your papers, madam!"

"She doesn't have any!" blurted out the boy.

"Why not?" pressed the policeman.

"She ate them!"

Sid shot Eric a look that said, "Why on earth did you just say that?"

Eric shot Sid a look back that said, "I don't know."

"Why would anyone eat their own **IDENTITY PAPERS?**" asked the incredulous policeman.

"If you were very hungry," guessed the boy.

"And you enjoyed the taste of cardboard!" added Sid. "It's quite nice with some brown sauce!"

"Let me have a look at her," demanded the policeman, leaning down to Gertrude's face.

"Oh no! Don't lift her veil!" begged Eric.

"Why ever not?"

"She's not got her make-up on!" replied Sid. "She hates people seeing her without her make-up!"

"Britain comes first! Madam, would you please be kind enough to lift your veil?"

Being a gorilla, and not speaking English, Gertrude did nothing of the sort.

TOOT! TOOT! went the train again.

"I told you she wouldn't," said Sid.

The policeman was having no more of this nonsense.

He leaned down and lifted up the veil himself. Needless to say, he was shocked by what he saw. This big, hairy ape smiling back at him, offering a handful of cake.

"HURGH?" she asked.

" ARGH!"

screamed the policeman, taking a step back to hide behind the other. But he was scared too, and there began a game of who could hide behind who.

TOOT! TOOT!

That was the final whistle! The train began leaving the station!

"I am very sorry, officer, but we have to go!" shouted Sid over the noise of the engine.

The three then began chasing after the train.

"COME BACK HERE!" shouted the policeman.

"STOP IN THE NAME OF THE LAW!

HALT THAT

TRAIN!"

CHAPTER 39

KEEP THE SHOE

CLASSIFIED

The policemen blew their whistles.

TWOOOOT!

There were shouts and the sounds of boot steps...

"STOP THEM!"

"CATCH THEM!"

"GORILLA ON THE LOOSE!"

STOMP! STOMP! STOMP!

...as our three heroes were chased along the platform. They didn't dare turn round and look. Just to make it on to the train would be a miracle.

Sid was really struggling to keep up on his old tin legs...

CLINK! CLANK! CLUNK!

...especially as he was pushing the wheelchair too.

Eric was helping push, but Gertrude was HEAVY! And all that fruit-and-nut cake had made her HEAVIER!

293

"At this rate, we're going to miss the train!" gasped Sid, huffing and puffing.

"Then we have no choice. GERTRUDE! RUN!" shouted Eric, pulling the gorilla up to her feet.

The wheelchair toppled over on to the platform.

THUNK!

Happily, it landed right in the policemen's way, delaying their pursuit for a few crucial seconds.

"BLAST!"

Gertrude could run surprisingly fast, though, of course, being a gorilla, she had the strangest gait – this low lollop that looked most unlike that of a person. Still in her wedding dress/net curtains, she raced to

the back of the train, and hung on to the handle at the end. Eric ran after her, reached out and clung on to Gertrude's huge hairy hand. Then, with his other hand, the boy reached back for Sid.

"You go without me!" the old man shouted heroically, now some way behind. **"Save Gertrude!"**

"No!" said Eric. "You are coming with us! Come on, Gertrude! We have to save him!"

He yanked on the animal's hand, and they leaped down off the moving train back on to the platform.

THUD!

"Get on her back, Uncle Sid!" ordered the boy.

"I can't…!" spluttered the man.

"Just do it! She'll give you a ride, won't you, Gertrude?"

The gorilla nodded and hauled him on to her back. Then she took a running leap on to the end of the train.

WHOOSH!
THUMP!

Once there, she climbed on to the roof.

"I really could get used to this!" exclaimed Sid.

The boy, still on the platform, chased after the now speeding train.

Just as Eric could feel the policemen breathing down his neck, he copied what he'd just seen Gertrude do. He took a running jump…

WHOOSH!
THUMP!

…and just managed to grab hold of the handle at the back of the train.

However, one of the policemen grabbed on to his foot.

"GOTCHA!" he shouted.

Eric wiggled and waggled and woggled* his

---

* *Check the definition in your* **Walliamsictionary**, *the least trusted book of words in the world.*

ankle as much as he could.

WIGGLE! WAGGLE! WOGGLE!

Just as he'd hoped, his shoe came off in the policeman's hand.

As the train chugged out of the station, the policeman was left standing at the very end of the platform holding a small shoe. He threw it to the ground in frustration.

THWACK!

And stamped on it for good measure.

STOMP!

"NOOOO!" he shouted.

Eric clambered up on to the roof of the train, struggling with his footing as he only had one shoe on. Despite this minor setback, the boy was in triumphant spirits. He turned round and waved back to the policeman.

"YOU CAN KEEP THE SHOE!" he shouted.

From behind him on the roof of the train, he heard Sid shout, "DUCK!"

Eric looked left and right, "You keep saying 'duck'. But I can't see any ducks anywhere!"

"NO! WE ARE GOING INTO A TUNNEL! DUCK!"

The boy turned round to see that the train was indeed

going into a low tunnel. Gertrude and Sid were already lying flat on the top of the train. If Eric didn't act fast, he would smash straight into the brick arch.

But he was so terrified he felt

frozen to the spot...

CHAPTER 40

STUNNED NUNS

Sid yanked Eric's ankle to topple him over. The boy landed on the top of the train with a…

THUD!

Eric shut his eyes tight as he felt the arch of the tunnel skim over his head.

VROOSH!

The boy was lucky to be alive, and he knew it. In moments, the dark turned to light as the train galloped out of the tunnel.

It was now trundling across a railway bridge over the River Thames, heading south. The three had to find the third-class carriage. So, taking a windswept Gertrude in their hands, her wedding dress blowing wildly, they tiptoed across the roof to the front of the train. Between each carriage there was a wide gap to leap over. Not so difficult for an ape, or a small, sprightly boy. However, this was a huge challenge for an old man with tin legs.

"I'm not sure about this!" spluttered Sid.

"You can do it!" assured Eric. "Just take a running jump!"

The old man shook his head, but took a few steps back before doing his best to leap from one carriage to another.

"ARGH!" cried Sid as he lost his footing and fell down the gap.

CLANK!

Eric just managed to grab the old man's hand to stop him falling on to the tracks!

"I'VE GOT YOU!" said the boy.

But the old man's hand was slipping out of Eric's.

"YES! BUT FOR HOW LONG?"

To make matters worse, it was hard to see a thing. Thick plumes of smoke were chugging from the engine at the front as the train began to reach its top speed.

CHUG! CHUG! CHUG!

Spotting her friends were in trouble, Gertrude leaned down from the top of the train and reached out a helping hand. The gorilla was a good deal stronger than Eric, or indeed anyone. Grabbing Sid's other hand, she yanked him back on top of the carriage. He landed with a…

THUMP!

"Are you all right?" asked Eric.

"Just a bit winded!" replied Sid.

"Gertrude! Let's grab a hand each," said the boy, miming.

The gorilla nodded. She was a clever girl! Now with Sid in the middle, the three leaped over the wide gaps between the train carriages together.

"WHEE!" exclaimed the old man, feeling like a child again for the first time in half a century. It was as if he were a toddler being swung by his parents.

Soon the three had reached the front of the train.

"Now we need to find an empty compartment," said Sid.

"Lower me down the side and I can look through the windows!" replied the boy.

Gertrude and Sid held on to Eric's ankles as he was lowered down to look through the first compartment window.

A group of stunned nuns looked up from their Bible-reading. The boy smiled at them and gestured to be pulled up.

The next compartment was full of children. They all had name tags round their necks, no doubt being evacuated to the countryside. The children smiled and waved and looked super-excited to see the upside-down boy outside the window. Eric waved before gesturing to be pulled back up.

"Third time lucky!" he said as Sid and Gertrude lowered him to look through the window of the next compartment.

"YES!" exclaimed the boy. "This one is empty!"

Still upside down, Eric slid the window open and swung through it. He landed in a crumpled heap on the floor of the compartment.

THUNK!

Next, he leaned out of the window to help first Gertrude, and then Sid inside. The old man caught his trousers on the door handle, and they whipped down.

WHIP!

"Not again!" he exclaimed as his wrinkly bottom stuck out of the window.

Eric hauled him inside, and Sid hastily yanked up his trousers.

Breathless, windswept, and covered in soot from all the smoke, the three were at last slumped on seats. Eric closed the window...

SHUNT!

...and they all let out a giant sigh of relief.

"HUH!"

The wind had blustered Gertrude's wedding dress all over the place. She looked as if she'd been dragged through a hedge backwards. Her furry face, arms and legs were now clearly on display.

"Oops!" remarked the boy.

"Oops indeed!" echoed Sid.

Eric looked out of the door on the other side of the

compartment that led on to the carriage corridor. To his horror, he could see a lady approaching, pushing a tea trolley.

"The tea lady's coming! We have to get Gertrude straightened out! Now!"

As Gertrude looked on, confused, the pair set to work, pulling and straightening the bits of old net curtain that made up the wedding dress.

"Sorry!" said the boy. "It's not that you are not beautiful!"

Gertrude beamed back, puckering up her lips for a kiss.

"Not now!" the boy hissed.

He just managed to yank the veil over Gertrude's face…

SWISH!

…when the door to the compartment swung open…

CHAPTER 41

BOTTOM RASPBERRY

CLASSIFIED

"Anything from the trolley, dears?" chirped the smiley old tea lady as she wobbled about in the compartment with the movement of the train. With one of her plump hands, she gestured to the impressive selection of sandwiches, cakes and biscuits.

Instantly, Gertrude's gloved hand shot out from under her dress. As Sid and Eric looked on aghast, the gorilla helped herself to huge handfuls of everything.

SWIPE!

She began stuffing all the food into her face, making the most appalling noises as she ate.

"SLURP! GLURP! FLURP!"

The tea lady looked on in horror. Within seconds, this newlywed had demolished just about everything on the trolley and was still going!

"SLURP! GLURP! FLURP!"

"I am so sorry," began Sid. "My wife didn't have anything to eat at the wedding reception and she's starving."

"I can see that!" said the tea lady, now wobbling in shock as much as the train. "My goodness, she'll eat you out of house and home!"

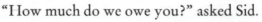

"How much do we owe you?" asked Sid.

The tea lady was trying to add up all the items, but they were disappearing off her trolley quicker than she could count them. To make it harder for her, Gertrude was now swiping the tea, milk and sugar too, and pouring them down her throat.

"Let's call it ten bob!"

Ten shillings was a lot of money. It was also all that Sid had on him, so he handed it over with a weak smile.

306

"Maybe it would be best to leave us the trolley," Eric piped up. "Just in case she finds any crumbs!"

"You promise she won't eat that too?" huffed the tea lady. "I would get into big trouble if my trolley got eaten."

"We promise," said Eric.

"I don't want to come back and see any bite marks!"

"It's safe with us!"

"I'll be back for it in a jiffy…"

Eric and Sid hurriedly helped themselves to anything that Gertrude hadn't already scoffed. Eric chose a Scotch egg, and Sid a jam doughnut. However, just as they raised them to their mouths to eat, Gertrude's hand snatched them away and stuffed them in hers. Quite what a Scotch egg and a doughnut tasted like eaten together was anyone's guess, but the gorilla seemed happy enough. After she'd wolfed (or rather 'gorillaed'*) them down, she let out the most deafening **BURP.**

"BuUUUUUuUuUuRRrrrRRRP!"

---

* Your **Walliamsictionary** has this and billions of other made-up words.

Her veil flapped up with the force of it.

It was quite the eggiest, sausagiest, mustardiest, jammiest, doughnuttiest **burp** you could ever have the misfortune to smell.

BURP CLOUD

EGG

SUGAR

MUSTARD

SAUSAGES

BREADCRUMBS

JAM

DOUGHNUTS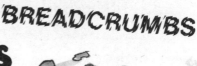

Eric leaped up to open the window.

SHUNT!

But the air gushing in just swirled the burp around and the smell went right up his nose.

WHOOSH!

"YUCK!"

Instantly, he closed the window and slumped back down. He and Sid had been up all night and were exhausted. They leaned back on the headrests and closed their eyes. No sooner were they drifting off to sleep than they were awoken by a deafening noise.

"**PFFFFFFFT!**" came a sound not unlike one of the raspberries that Gertrude would blow.

Except this was no raspberry. This was a bottom raspberry.

A gorilla burp is bad enough, but a gorilla bottom burp is something else. You need a gas mask to survive it.

BOTTOM-BURP CLOUD

EGG

CHEESE

SAUSAGE ROLLS

JAM

MARMALADE

SUGAR

RAISINS

MUSTARD

BROWN SAUCE

BUTTER

BACON

BREADCRUMBS

TEA

"I think Gertrude needs to use the lavatory!" announced a choking Sid, his eyes watering from the stink. "As a matter of some urgency!"

"YOU DON'T SAY!" exclaimed the boy sarcastically.

"I'd better take her down the corridor to the loo!"

"Yes! Right away!"

Eric pulled back the veil to have a proper look at the gorilla's face. By the squirming expression, the boy knew they didn't have much time.

"I don't think you're going to make it all the way to the toilet!" exclaimed the boy.

"Oh no! She's going to spoil her lovely wedding dress."

"There is one thing we can do!"

"What's that?" asked Sid.

"Stick her bottom out of the window!"

"BUT—!" protested the old man.

"PFFFFFFFFFFFFFFFFFFFFFT!"

It was another gorilla bottom burp, even more thunderous than the last.

"Come on, old girl," said Sid as they helped the gorilla into position.

Eric slid down the window.

SHUNT!

Like a cannon firing so did the gorilla's bottom.

BANG!

Something brown and missile-shaped shot out of the window.

WHIZZ!

It zoomed over some trees, landing in a farmer's field, where it exploded.

KABOOM!

It caused a herd of cattle to scatter.

"MOOO!"

"MOOO!"

"MOOO!"

The tea lady came back to witness the pair holding the bride's bottom out of the window.

"As promised!" chirped the boy. "No bite marks on your trolley!"

"Is she all right?" she asked.

"Yes. Just enjoying the country air!"

The now incredibly wobbly lady grabbed her trolley and trundled off down the corridor at speed.

"Now, let's all settle down and try to get some rest before we reach Bognor Regis," suggested Sid.

Each laid a head on the gorilla's shoulder, and she cuddled them both tight. In no time, the exhausted trio were fast asleep.

"ZZZZ! ZZZZ! ZZZZ!"

Little did they know who would be waiting for them

when they woke up...

CHAPTER 42

LOST PROPERTY

SCREECH!

The train's brakes screeching as it arrived into Bognor Regis station woke Eric up with a start. Peering out of the window on the platform side, he could see a gaggle of policemen waiting there. One was even holding a giant net.

The policemen at Victoria station must have called ahead. Now there was **no escape!**

Or was there?

The train came to a juddering halt as Eric began desperately shaking Sid and Gertrude to wake them up.

"Wake up! Wake up!"

In moments, both had come to, Gertrude letting out a terrific yawn.

"UUURRRGGGHHHEEEHHH!"

"Look!" hissed Eric, pointing out of the window at

313

what looked like the entire Bognor Regis Constabulary out in force.

"Oh no," replied Sid.

"We'll have to sneak out this side!" said Eric.

He climbed out of the window and landed on the railway line.

KERTUNK!

This was **DANGEROUS** with a capital **D!**

If another train arrived, he would be squished in an instant.

Eric's eyes darted left and right. Checking that the coast was clear, he helped the other two down from the train. Gertrude pushed Sid's bottom up and out, and then leaped down on to the line herself. Next, the three tiptoed over the track and heaved themselves up the platform on the other side. Peering into the carriage windows they could see the policemen swarming on to the train, searching for them.

The three slid round a corner on the platform, and came across a little office with a sign on the door which read:

It was deserted. No doubt all the station staff had also been enlisted to look out for the three runaways.

"Let's hide in here!" hissed Eric.

They slipped inside, closing the door silently behind them.

The office was a **treasure trove** of things folks had left behind at the station over the years. There were umbrellas, bowler hats, books, buckets and spades, rubber duckies, suitcases, kites, deckchairs, dollies, teddy bears, a beach ball, a globe, a pram and even a stuffed cat. Gertrude whipped back her veil, her face a picture of delight. Here were lots of new toys to play with! Immediately, she began bouncing the beach ball...

BOING! BOING! BOING!

...twirled the umbrella as if she were doing a song-and-dance number...

SWISH!

...and took a great big bite out of a bowler hat.

MUNCH!

"Stop that, Gertrude!" hissed Eric. "We may need this stuff. We can use some of these clothes as disguises!"

"Good thinking!" said Sid, reaching for one of the suitcases from a shelf. "The policemen at Victoria station would have given detailed descriptions of us. We have to lose this wedding-party look at once!"

"And now that we don't have the wheelchair, maybe we can use **this!**" suggested the boy, holding the handle of the pram.

"A pram?"

"It's huge. It must be for twins!"

"Or one **very big baby?**" said Sid slyly.

They both turned to look at Gertrude. The gorilla was not enjoying the taste of the bowler hat at all, but she carried on eating.

MUNCH! MUNCH! MUNCH!

"Do you think she'd even fit in the pram?" asked Eric.

Gertrude frowned and shook her head.

"Well, if you think you can persuade her!" remarked Sid.

The gorilla crossed her arms as if in a **ginormous** huff!

"Mmm. I'll try," replied the boy. He smiled at his furry friend, who frowned back. Her forehead wrinkled like a walnut.

"Good luck!" joked Sid.

"There must be some way to bribe her!"

"Well, we know she loves her food! Maybe we can find something in here, and we need good outfits for us!"

They opened a big battered suitcase. It was jammed full of **long, flowery** dresses.

"Oh no!" said Eric.

"I'm sure they'll have your size!" chuckled Sid.

"But—"

"It'll be the perfect disguise! The police aren't looking for two ladies with a baby! Are they?"

"No," agreed the boy.

"Come on, then! Let's take some other bits and bobs to change into as soon as we are out of the station! And you need a shoe!"

"That I do!"

After a short while, the door of the lost property office slowly opened.

CREAK!

Sid stepped out first. He was wearing a **long, flowery** yellow dress, topped off with white silk gloves, sunglasses and a sunhat. The old man hid his beard behind a lady's fan.

Next it was Eric's turn. He was sporting a lady's pink

bathing costume, a **flowery** purple bathing hat, goggles and a rubber ring round his waist.

Both pulled out the huge pram, which only just fitted through the door.

Inside the pram, hidden under a number of colourful beach towels, was Gertrude. The old gorilla looked like the most unusual newborn baby you'd ever seen. She was sucking on a huge stick of Bognor Regis rock Eric had found her.

"SLURP!
SLURP!
SLURP!"

It was just what he'd needed to tempt her into the pram, and so much **tastier** than a bowler hat.

With just the right swagger, the three waltzed straight past the throng of waiting policemen on the platform, who watched them with great curiosity.

Would the police stop them?

Was the game up?

Not yet!

The policemen studied them for a while, before turning their attention to the other passengers who were coming and going from the station.

Now there was just the ticket barrier between our heroes and freedom.

CHAPTER 43

TWITCHING MOUSTACHE

CLASSIFIED

Standing to attention at the station's ticket barrier was a little man with a big moustache. He looked, in a word, officious.

"Tickets, please!" he barked, his moustache twitching as he spoke.

Sid produced the three tickets and handed them over with what he thought was a feminine flourish.

The little man inspected the tickets closely, and then tore them in two.

Sid cooed in his most ladylike voice, "Thank you, my good man. Well, if everything is in order, we must be on our way to enjoy the sights and sounds of Bognor Regis!"

"STOP!" replied the ticket inspector.

Lady Sid and Lady Eric shared a nervous glance. Oh no! They were done for!

320

"I love babies!" said the little man. "Mind if I take a peek?"

"She's very shy!" huffed Lady Sid.

"Oh, just a quick peek!"

"She's sleeping!" hissed Lady Eric.

"Don't worry! I won't wake her!" replied the little man.

With that, he pulled back the beach towel. He revealed a smiling Gertrude, sucking on her stick of rock.

"SLURP! SLURP! SLURP!"

A look of **horror** spread across the man's face. His moustache was now twitching like a kite in a storm. It looked as if it might fly off his face at any moment.

"Pretty as a peach, isn't she?" chirped Lady Eric. "Now, come along, baby!"

With the man still frozen to the spot in shock, the two pushed the pram out of Bognor Regis station. As soon as they turned a corner, they picked up as much speed as they could.

RITTLE! RATTLE! RUTTLE!

The pair then leaped on the back of the pram as it bounced along the pavement from the station into the town.

BOINK! BOINK! BOINK!

"We did it!" exclaimed Sid.

"We certainly did!" agreed the boy.

"SLURP! SLURP! SLURP!" went Baby Gertrude on her stick of rock.

They were dressed perfectly for a delightful summer's day at the beach.

Such a shame it was December.

They had escaped into the charming little seaside town of Bognor Regis. **Seaview Towers** wasn't far away.

They had no clue of the

terrible danger that was

lurking there.

PART FOUR
A MONSTROUS TYRANNY

CHAPTER | 44 |

STRICTLY FORBIDDEN

Bognor Regis was all but deserted at this time of year. It was a summer seaside town and, like most summer seaside towns, it looked bleak in winter.

Sid had come here for many of the summers of his boyhood. He remembered the zigzag route through the little streets to the seafront with ease. However, Eric had never been out of London. The boy marvelled at his first-ever sight of the sea. He looked out in wonder as giant waves crashed on the beach.

Gertrude sat up in her pram and stared out at the sea. Not liking water, she shook her head, and went back to sucking on her stick of rock.

"SLURP!"

"I love the seaside!" exclaimed the boy, shivering from the cold. "But I'm not sure Gertrude here is so keen!"

Just then a gust of wind caught Sid's long flowery dress, whipping it up over his head.

WHIP!

Now anyone could see his undercrackers!

"I'm not sure any of us are dressed for this weather!" muttered the old man. "Let's get changed."

Behind them was a long row of painted beach huts. They found one with a door that was unlocked and bustled the pram inside.

The dresses had proved the perfect disguise to pass through Bognor Regis station, but now some more practical clothing was needed. They had swiped some coats, shirts, shoes and trousers from the lost property office and stuffed them into the basket under the pram. As quickly as they could, they got changed. But there was still a big question looming…

"What about Baby Gertrude?" asked the boy.

The pair peeked into the pram. The gorilla had finished her stick of rock. Now she was sucking her thumb, snoring away, sound asleep.

" Z Z Z Z ! Z Z Z Z ! Z Z Z Z ! "

"She looks happy enough," replied Sid. "Let's leave the old girl to sleep. It's still quite a walk to the guesthouse, and if we get her out of the pram someone will spot her."

"Yes. That gorilla walk is a bit of a giveaway!"

"It's how I used to walk when I had an accident!"

"HA! HA!" they chuckled together.

Gertrude stirred in her pram.

"URGH!"

Sid put his finger to his lips, and whispered, "It's best if we don't wake her!"

As quietly as he could, Eric opened the door to the beach hut. First, checking the coast was clear (literally, the coast), they gently pushed Gertrude in the pram along the seafront. After a long, blustery walk along the coast they spotted their destination.

Seaview Towers.

The spooky-looking Gothic building sat on a cliff overlooking the sea. Its dark grey bricks were crumbling after decades of being battered by storms. There were turrets on the roof that looked like ones you might find on a castle. Some of the windows must have been broken, as the glass had been boarded up with wood.

A sign at the bottom of the hill that led up to the cliff read:

SEAVIEW TOWERS
CLOSED.
ENTRY IS STRICTLY
FORBIDDEN

"Here we are," said Sid, straining as he helped push the sleeping beauty up the hill. "It'll be the perfect place for us to hide out until things quieten down."

As they made their way along the garden path, Eric was certain he saw a curtain twitch.

"Uncle Sid!" he hissed. **"LOOK!"**

"What?"

"Something moved in the window," said the boy, pointing.

The old man trained his eyes on the window, but now there was nothing there. All the lights were off, and all the curtains were drawn.

"I think you might be imagining things, young lad. This place is closed."

"I saw what I saw, Uncle Sid," protested the boy.

They made the rest of their way up the long path without another word.

The sky was a swirl of black clouds. Thunder and lightning struck.

BOOM!

SNAP!

CHAPTER | 45 |
THE WILLIES

CLASSIFIED

Finally, our heroes reached the top of the hill just as the rain began to lash down.

"This place brings back fond memories," began Sid. "Playing in the garden, looking for frogs in that pond. And look," he said, pointing out to sea, "from here on a clear day you can see for miles. Oh, I used to love that. My dad had a pair of binoculars, and I would sit for hours and watch all the navy ships going back and forth from Portsmouth Harbour. Happy days."

"They sound it."

"They were. Shame Seaview Towers is all closed down now. Still, it's good news for us, being on the run! Right! I'd better stop jabbering on! We need to get shelter from the storm. Let's force one of those windows open."

The boy shook his head. "There might be someone in there."

"Who?"

"I don't know. An old hobo or someone."

"There's no one in there!"

"I say let's knock on the door just in case anyone is at home."

"All right! All right!" conceded Sid. "Have it your way! Let's knock on the door."

The rain was washing away cobwebs that looked as if they'd been there for years. In the centre of the front door was a rusty old knocker.

Sid sighed and banged it.

RAT! TAT! **TAT!**

Nothing.

"See, no one's at home!" said the man.

Eric knocked on the door again.

RAT! **TAT! TAT!**

"Nothing! Come on, let's force open a window!"

"Shush!" shushed the boy.

"What?"

Despite the sound of the rain falling, Eric was certain he could hear footsteps on the other side of the door.

"There's someone inside! I swear!"

"Nonsense!" Sid shook his head, but bent down to

put his ear to the letterbox. He nodded his head. The boy was right!

Eric gulped in fear.

"GULP!"

It was hard to tell how many people were in there, but it was definitely more than one, as the footsteps echoed from different sides of the building.

SHUNT! SHUNT! SHUNT!

The next sound was that of locks being unlocked.

CLICK!
CLOCK!
CLACK!

The front door opened just a sliver. A rusty old metal chain prevented it from going any further. Half the face of an elderly lady, her blonde hair and glamorous make-up perfectly in place, loomed in the crack.

"State your business!" she demanded.

There was a trace of a

foreign accent, but it was hard to place it exactly.

"Oh, we, erm, just wondered if you had a room, please?" spluttered a shocked Sid.

"**Seaview Towers** is completely full! There are no vacancies here whatsoever!" she snapped.

"But we have nowhere else to go," he pleaded.

"That is not my concern. You must leave at once! Do you hear me? At once!"

"Bertha!" hissed a voice from out of view.

"Yes, Helene?" replied the first woman.

"Come here this instant!".

There were two of them! And the one they hadn't seen yet was definitely in charge!

The door was slammed in Sid and Eric's faces.

BANG!

What sounded like a heated argument between the two went on for quite a while inside. It was hard for Sid or Eric to make out what was being said, as it didn't sound as if they were speaking in English.

"Maybe we should make a run for it?" hissed Eric, unable to ignore the feeling of deep unease in his tummy.

"We're stuck here," replied Sid. He looked back over the little town of Bognor Regis being battered by the storm. "If we go back to London, then Gertrude here is a goner!"

Eric had a peep into the pram. The sleeping beauty was still sleeping beautifully.

"ZZZZ! ZZZZ! ZZZZ!"

The boy smiled at the sight, before a sense of dread came over him. "But this place, Uncle Sid... It gives me the..."

But, sooner than Eric could say "willies", the chain on the door was hurriedly taken off...

KERCHANG!

...and the door opened wide.

CREAK!

Now not one but two ladies were revealed in the doorway of **Seaview Towers.**

They were identical twins and made a startling sight. These two ancient faces, with bright pink lipstick, rouge on their cheeks and aquamarine eyeshadow painted over their eyelids, looked out of place in this dusty old ruin.

Their hair must have been dyed as it was the colour of gold. It made them look like film stars from the silent era. They wore matching cream blouses, each with a string of pearls round their neck. Black pencil skirts and patent-leather high-heeled shoes completed the look. They were by far the most glamorous pair in Bognor Regis.

"You are in luck!" chirped the second one. "We have just had a cancellation!"

Then in unison they both beckoned their guests inside with the words, "Welcome to **Seaview Towers**."

Eric felt sick with nerves.

Something was very wrong here.

CHAPTER | 46 |
COBWEBS

CLASSIFIED

Seaview Towers was just as rundown on the inside as it was on the outside. Pushing the pram inside as gently as they possibly could so as not to wake Gertrude, Sid and Eric instantly thought that the guesthouse couldn't have had a visitor for some time.

The chairs, tables and shelves in the hallway were inches thick with dust.

Mould splattered over the walls like a disease.

Long dangly cobwebs hung from the ceiling.

A vase of dead flowers stood stiffly in a bone-dry vase on a counter.

As soon as the visitors were inside, the twins hastily shut the door.

BANG!

Then they locked, double-locked and triple-locked it, making sure to take the key with them.

CLOCK! CLACK! CLICK!

"Welcome! Welcome!" began the second sister. "Our home is your home. We couldn't be more delighted that you chose to stay here."

"I used to come here as a boy," replied Sid.

"Ah! Delight of delights! Welcome back! Your names, if you please…"

"I'm Sid."

"And I am Eric."

"Sidney and Eric. Wonderful! Wonderful! And what, pray, is the name of your baby?"

"What baby?" replied Sid, not thinking.

Eric elbowed him in his ribs.

"Ouch!"

"The one in the pram?" reminded the lady, with a suspicious look in her eye.

"Oh, that baby!" said Sid, recovering quickly. "Her name is… Gertrude! Baby Gertrude. But please don't disturb her, because she is sleeping!"

"Very well. May I ask whose baby it is? Forgive me, but you look too young, and you look too old to have a baby."

Now it was Sid and Eric's turn to look at each other.

"Erm, it's my little sister!" lied the boy. "This is my great-uncle. We were evacuated out of London because of the bombing."

"Ah! The bombing!" exclaimed the second twin. "Those Nazis will never, ever stop!" she added, smiling. "Oh! Please, forgive our manners! Permit us to introduce ourselves! My name is Madame Brown."

"My name is also Madame Braun," said the other.

"Braun?" repeated Sid.

"Brown!" snapped the scarier one. "Please forgive my younger sister's very slight accent. We are not from Bognor…"

"…or Regis!"

"Bognor Regis!" she snapped again, this time smacking her twin sister's hand **hard.**

THWACK!

The other sister seemed used to this as she didn't cry out. However, it was painful enough for her eyes to glisten with tears.

"As you can see, we are **twin sisters!**" said the other one.

"No! I'd never have guessed!" joked Sid, trying to lighten the mood.

The ladies were not the least bit amused.

"As I was saying before the interruption, as we are twin sisters both named Brown," began the other one, "I will permit you two gentlemen to refer to me as Madame Bertha."

"And you can call me Madame Helene!"

"Thank you, Madame Bertha. Thank you, Madame Helene," replied Eric. He was trying to be as polite as possible after Sid's joke had fallen so **flat.**

"You are very fortunate that we have just the one room here at **Seaview Towers** that is vacant!" said Helene. "Please follow me," she added, leading them up the staircase.

Eric and Sid looked at each other as if to say, "STAIRS!"

"You can leave the pram in the hallway, and carry the baby up to your room," said Bertha.

"Erm… well… You see… No…" spluttered Sid.

"We wouldn't want to clutter up your hallway with the pram!" leaped in Eric.

Together he and Sid hoisted the **humongously** heavy gorilla in the pram up the flight of stairs. They took each step as carefully as they could, desperate not to wake Gertrude from her slumber. However, the load was so intense that in no time they were both sweating and shaking.

"The baby is heavy, no?" asked Bertha.

"Just normal baby size!" squeaked Eric, clearly straining.

CLINK! CLANK! CLUNK! went the old man's tin legs on the stairs.

"What is that clanking sound?" remarked Helene.

"It's just my tin legs," replied Sid. "I lost mine in the First World War."

"How very careless of you," purred Bertha.

The old man shook his head, before he and Eric finally reached the landing at the top of the stairs.

"This is your room!" began Bertha.

"Number **THIRTEEN,**" added Helene.

"Unlucky for some!" joked Sid.

"Let's pray it is not," said Bertha with a smile as she unlocked and opened the door.

CREAK!

The bedroom was full of dust, dirt and cobwebs. There was a strong musty smell of damp. It seemed as if no one had been in here for quite a while. There were two single beds, a desk and a chair. The curtains were drawn, so Madame Bertha glided over to the window and opened them. This sent a cloud of dust bursting into the room.

WHOOF!

It made Eric and Sid cough and splutter.

"HUH!"

"URGH!"

"Please do not spread germs. We will bring you a pot of hot tea presently," announced Bertha.

"Please don't go to any trouble," replied Sid.

"It is our pleasure," purred Bertha. "You must drink up the tea. It will warm you from the rain and cold."

"I don't really like tea," said Eric.

"You will drink the tea," she said again.

This sent a shiver down the boy's spine.

As he and Sid pushed the pram through the doorway, it became clear it was too wide and got stuck.

SCRITCH!

"Do you need assistance?" asked Helene.

"We may not look it, but we are both as strong as oxen!" added Bertha.

"We can manage!" said Eric. With a coordinated

shove, they just managed to squeeze the pram through the doorway. Not without waking up Gertrude, though, who suddenly made a loud noise...

"HEE-HAW!"

"What was that?" demanded Bertha.

"HEEE-HAAW!"

"The baby just needs winding!" lied Eric.

"Thank you so much!" added Sid, hurrying the ladies out of the room and slamming the bedroom door in their faces.

SHONT!

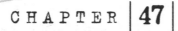

CHAPTER | 47 |

BOING! BOING! BOING!

The gorilla sat up in her pram, taking in her new surroundings. Looking around the damp, dirty old bedroom of **Seaview Towers,** it seemed Gertrude didn't like it that much.

She blew a raspberry. "**PFFT!**" That was her verdict on the place!

Eric gave her a stroke on the head, and Gertrude nuzzled up to him. He held her tight and kissed her.

"I'm sorry this is all a bit strange, Gertrude, but it's for the best."

In turn, she grabbed his head with her huge furry hand and gave him a smacker too!

"*MWAH!*"

"HELP!" hissed Eric. The gorilla was holding him a little too tight and she was not letting go.

"Come along now, old girl!" ordered Sid. "We know

you love Eric, but let him breathe!"

Gertrude released her grip and set the boy free. She leaped out of the pram and landed on the worn carpet with a **THOMP!**

"SHUSH!" urged Eric.

The room was dark and dingy, so the boy flicked on the light switch.

FLICK!

The bare bulb hanging from the ceiling instantly exploded.

BANG!

"This place has really gone off," remarked Sid.

"You don't say!"

"**PFFFFT!**" agreed Gertrude.

"But at least we are all safe," said Sid.

"But are we?" asked the boy.

"How do you mean?"

"Those two ladies. They're peculiar."

"This is a British seaside town! British seaside towns are full of peculiar people!"

"Not just peculiar! Peculiar peculiar! All that nonsense they said about Seaview Towers being full. We didn't see or hear a soul."

"No, but there might be a few guests dotted around in their rooms, having an afternoon snooze."

"Then why did it say on the sign that 'entry is strictly forbidden'?" asked Eric, clearly not convinced.

The conversation was interrupted by the sound of bouncing.

BOING!

Gertrude was bouncing up and down on the bed on her bottom.

BOING! BOING! BOING!

"No, Gertrude! Please!" begged the boy.

But it was no use. The gorilla was having fun, and nothing and no one was going to get in the way of that. Now Gertrude had pushed herself up to her feet and was jumping up and down on the bed as if it were a trampoline.

BOING! BOING! BOING!

Another dust cloud, this time from the bed, burst into the room.

WHOOF!

The gorilla's eyes widened with delight.

347

This was COOL!

"WHOOPY WHOOPY DOO!" she whooped.

"NO!" barked Eric, grabbing her hand and bringing her to a stop. "Please! Please! You're going to give the game away. Please, Gertrude, just have a nice lie-down."

"PFFFFFT!" She blew a raspberry into the boy's face, covering him once again in gorilla spittle.

Eric smiled and wiped his face clean with his shirtsleeve, before pacing over to the bedroom door.

"Where are you off to?" asked Sid.

"To investigate, of course!" replied Eric.

"Investigate what?"

"The twins. They're up to something. I know it."

"Be careful!"

"I will!"

"And tell them not to be too long with that tea! I am parched!"

Eric put his ear up against the keyhole. Outside, the floorboards were creaking.

CREAK!

It sounded as if someone might be lurking just on the other side of the door. So Eric tiptoed back over to the bed.

"Gertrude! I need your help," hissed the boy.

He took her hands in his and heaved her up to her feet, before leading her over to the bedroom window.

As quietly as he could, he opened it.

SHUNT!

Then Eric gestured for the gorilla to turn round and he leaped on her back.

"NO!" mimed Sid, desperately shaking his head.

Eric put his fingers up to his lips, miming,

"SHUSH!"

The gorilla knew what to do. She climbed out of the window with the boy on her back, and together they disappeared out into the **raging storm.**

CHAPTER | 48 |

DEAD EYES

CLASSIFIED

Using the network of ledges and drainpipes on the outside of **Seaview Towers,** Eric and Gertrude went about their detective work.

The twins were up to something.

But what?

The storm was whipping the guesthouse without mercy. The rain had made the building slippery. The journey round the outside of the top floor was DOUBLY DANGEROUS, so Eric held on tight to his furry friend's back. As Gertrude clambered around, Eric peered in through the grimy windows. The curtains may have been drawn, but there were gaps or holes in them through which he could see.

Bedroom after bedroom, many of which had windows boarded up with wood, was empty. In fact, judging by the cobwebs that stretched out from floor to ceiling, it was clear no visitors had stayed in any of these rooms for some time.

So why had the twins lied and said that the guesthouse was full?

Continuing climbing round the top floor of the building, Gertrude led Eric to the one room that had a light on.

"**Good work, Gertrude!**" hissed the boy. "Hold on here for a moment!"

He peered in through the window. This bedroom was different from all the rest. It was opulently furnished and looked much neater and cleaner. There was a dressing table with a mirror, a chaise longue and two single beds.

"This must be the twins' bedroom!" said Eric.

Gertrude nodded her head in agreement.

Just then one of the twins breezed into the room.

Instantly the gorilla and the boy ducked their heads out of sight. However, Eric was higher up and could still just peek in through the window.

The lady went over to the dressing table. It was made of dark wood and looked antique. It came with a mirror and a stool for a lady to sit at and style her hair or apply her make-up. However, the lady's attention was focused

on the collection of ornate glass bottles on the tabletop. She was hurriedly sorting through them, clearly trying to find the right bottle. Finally, she found the one she wanted. It was a tall glass bottle with a silver eagle on top. It contained a red liquid. She grasped it in her hand and spun the mirror on the dressing table round.

Still clinging on to Gertrude's back outside the window, Eric's blood ran cold.

ICE COLD.

On one side, it was just a normal mirror, but on the other was an oil painting of someone. Someone who was the deadliest enemy of Britain, and the world.

Adolf Hitler.

In Nazi Germany, Hitler was known as the Führer, which meant "the leader". He was the evil dictator who had seized control of Germany and caused the deaths of countless innocent people.

Hitler was instantly recognisable by his small black moustache, his hair slicked over to one side and his cold, dead eyes. In the painting, he was wearing a military-style brown jacket with an armband on his left arm. It was red, with a white circle. In the middle of the white circle was a black symbol, like a cross, but with lines along the edges.

It was a swastika. The symbol of the Nazis. The Nazis wanted to create an evil empire around the world and enslave their enemies. Anyone who got in their way would be killed.

The old lady admired the painting for a while, then stood up and extended her right arm into the air. This was the Nazi salute.

"*Heil Hitler!*" she said, before spinning the picture back round to the mirror. Then she stopped dead in her tracks. Had she glimpsed something in the mirror while it spun? Had she seen the eyes of a small, wet boy or the forehead of a large, wet gorilla at the window?

CHAPTER | 49 |

GHOULISH GRINS

The lady turned to the window and began pacing towards it.

"DOWN!" hissed the boy.

Gertrude understood and shimmied down out of view, clinging on to the window ledge with her fingertips.

Above, Eric could just see the lady's breath fog the glass. Then she yanked the curtains closed.

SCHTUM!

Eric and Gertrude breathed a sigh of relief together.

"HURGH!"

Then Eric ordered, "UP!"

Gertrude clambered all the way up on to the roof. There Eric spotted something strange. There was an open hatch in the roof and poking out of it was the long lens of a telescope. But it wasn't pointing out to sea – it was pointing west along the coast.

"That way is Portsmouth!" exclaimed Eric. It was pointing where Sid had indicated earlier. "They must be spying on the British naval ships coming in and out. That's why this pair of Nazis are in Bognor Regis!"

This drew a blank with Gertrude, who shrugged.

"HUH?"

"Never mind! Let's go DOWN!"

Finding a nearby drainpipe, the pair slid all the way to the ground.

WHOOSH!
THUD! THUD!

Eric leaped off Gertrude's back. Taking her by the hand, he began spying through all the windows on the ground floor. At the first window, which was partly boarded up with wood, he peered through a crack at an empty living room. Three sofas were arranged in a triangular formation around what looked like a wireless. Wirelesses or radios came in all different shapes and sizes, but this was much larger than a usual wireless. What's more, it had been customised in various ways. Wires of all different colours sprang from it, and there were many more knobs and dials than on a normal wireless. Also, it had the tallest aerial you've ever seen.

This wireless looked designed to pick up much more than the usual BBC radio stations, as its reach seemed much greater. There were also two sets of headphones and a leather-bound notebook with a fountain pen to one side, presumably to write down what was heard.

"What are the twins listening in to?" asked the boy.

Again, the gorilla shrugged. "HUH?"

"Come on!" said Eric, holding Gertrude's hand in his.

Together, they moved on to explore some other rooms. Eric was sure there would be more clues hidden around the guesthouse.

They looked through another window into a dining room with a scattering of tables and chairs. Nothing suspicious there, aside from the fact that there were place settings for only two people, presumably the twins.

"I was right! There are no other guests!"

Next Eric and Gertrude peeped in through a tiny gap in the planks of wood boarding up a window and saw a library. It was stacked with shelves of dusty old leather-bound volumes. In the centre was a snooker table, covered with a sheet. On the top of that was spread a hugely detailed map. Eric was struggling to see, so Gertrude hoisted him higher.

"Thank you!"

Pushing his face right up against the window, Eric spotted that the map was of central London. He recognised the shape of the Thames as it snaked through the city centre.

"They've circled a building… It must be a **target!** But which one?" asked the boy, straining to make out which one. "Poop! I can't see it. Let's go!"

Gingerly, the pair tiptoed round the pond. Gorillas can't swim, and the last thing Eric wanted was his big, furry friend to fall in. The next window looked into the kitchen.

"Get down!" hissed Eric, pushing Gertrude's head out of sight.

One of the twins was at work preparing a tray of tea, when the other entered the room, carrying the perfume bottle from upstairs.

Then the ladies did the strangest thing.

As one lifted the lid on the teapot, the other poured some of the "perfume" in.

Eric's heart pounded in his chest.

"That isn't perfume!" he hissed to Gertrude. "It's **poison!** Once we knew they were here, they couldn't risk us telling anyone. That's why they let us in! Just so they could kill us!"

Gertrude picked up the alarm in the boy's tone of voice and her whole body shook.

"BRRR!"

The lid was closed on the teapot, and the twins grinned **ghoulishly.**

Then one picked up the tea tray, and together they left the room.

"If we don't get back up to the bedroom before Uncle Sid takes a sip, then…" Eric couldn't bear the thought. "UP! GERTRUDE! UP! WE NEED TO GO BACK TO THE BEDROOM! NOW!"

Once again, the boy leaped on to Gertrude's back.

"GO! GO! GO!"

Sensing the urgency in her friend's voice, the gorilla raced back up the building.

"FASTER! FASTER!" implored Eric.

The storm was now **ferocious.** The rain lashed down with such cruelty it was difficult for the ape to keep her eyes open. As she scrambled to the top floor, **DISASTER STRUCK.** Gertrude's hands slipped on the soaking-wet drainpipe. They fell backwards and began plummeting through the air...

"ARGH!"

"URGH!"

CHAPTER | 50 |

POISONED TEA

SPLOSH!

Eric and Gertrude crash-landed in the pond.

"HEEEEE!" screamed the gorilla. She couldn't swim, and began to flail around desperately.

"GERTRUDE! GERTRUDE! CALM DOWN!" cried Eric, who was underneath her.

But she wouldn't calm down. Her arms and legs were splaying everywhere.

SPLISH! SPLASH! SPLOSH!

"HEEEEE!"

There was a very big chance both of them could drown in this little pond.

With all his might, Eric pushed the gorilla up. Next, he placed her hands on the paving around the pond. Gertrude knew what to do and heaved herself out of the water. She then shook herself all over to try to get the water off her.

She spat an unlucky goldfish out of her mouth…

SPLURT!

…who luckily landed back in the pond.

SPLISH!

Meanwhile, Eric dragged himself out. A frog was squatting on his head, which he hastily returned to its home.

SPLASH!

"Gertrude, we've got to save Sid! It's too slippery for me to ride on your back. So let's go for it!"

With that, he took a few paces back and threw himself at the building. Using his best Gorilla Power, he scrambled up the side of the guesthouse at terrific speed. Gertrude was not far behind.

Once back at the bedroom, Eric hauled himself through the window. Then he reached out his hand to haul Gertrude in.

"You're both soaking wet!" exclaimed Sid, who was lying on the bed.

"It's a long story! Actually, it's a short story! We fell in the pond. **The end!**"

SHUNT! SHUNT! SHUNT!

It was the sound of footsteps coming along the hall.

"They're coming!" hissed the boy. "We have to get Gertrude back in the pram!"

Sid leaped up, and together he and Eric hoisted the damp ape into the pram and covered her with a towel.

Eric and Sid then took a running jump at the beds.

BOING!

The boy whipped the covers over himself to hide his wet clothes.

KNOCK! KNOCK! KNOCK!

"Your tea!" announced Helene, opening the door for Bertha, who was carrying the tray. They entered the room with their usual prim formality.

"Oh! Thank you, ladies!" chirped Sid, clearly looking forward to the tea. Of course, the old man had no idea it was **poisoned!**

"Please do drink it while it's nice and hot," said Bertha, placing the tray on the dusty desk. "It is murder out there!"

Bertha noticed that the window was wide open. She and her twin sister shared a suspicious look. In all the excitement, Eric had forgotten to shut it! He winced at his mistake.

"You must keep this window shut at all times!" said Bertha sternly. "You could catch your **death.**"

With her eyes, she indicated for Helene to shut the window, which she dutifully did.

"Where is the baby?" asked Helene.

"Oh, the baby's sleeping like a –" Eric struggled for a word, but it just didn't come – **"baby!"**

"Good, good," muttered Helene.

"WHOOP!" whooped the gorilla from the pram.

"Curious noise for a baby to make!" remarked

Bertha, more suspicious than ever. "May I see her?"

"Yes! Just as soon as she wakes up!"

"If she ever does! Well, you must excuse us! Myself and Madame Helene have some very important business to attend to. We remain, of course, at your loyal service. And don't let that tea get cold!"

With that, they both bowed their heads, spun on their heels and left the room.

"Uncle Sid!" hissed Eric. "They're trying to kill us!"

"**Kill us?**" spluttered the old man.

"Yes!"

Sid sat up in bed. "Let me just have a slurp of that tea!"

"NOOOOOOOOOOO!"

cried the boy.

CHAPTER 51

CRACKING THE CODE

CLASSIFIED

"What now?" spluttered Sid.

"The tea is **poisoned!**" exclaimed Eric.

The old man looked mightily disappointed and peered at the tea tray. "What about the biscuits?"

"I don't know! But I wouldn't touch them either if I were you."

"Shame! I'm famished! Why are those two old dears trying to kill us?"

"I reckon it's because we found them hiding here. They are Nazis!"

The man's eyes widened in horror. "Nazis? In Bognor Regis?"

"Yes!"

"How do you know?"

"I saw one of them give the Heil Hitler salute to a picture of Adolf Hitler."

"Well, that is a pretty strong sign of being a Nazi – I'll give you that!"

Gertrude sat up in the pram, and the boy helped get her dry by rubbing her with a towel.

As he did so, the gorilla searched his hair for nits and pulled a few out to eat.

"I never knew I had nits," remarked the boy.

"Well, don't knock it! They're a tasty treat for Gertrude," replied Sid.

Then his gaze was drawn to something out of the window.

"Hello? What's this?" he muttered to himself.

Sid got out of bed. A little unsteadily on his tin legs at first, he walked over to the window.

CLINK! CLANK! CLUNK!

"What's what?" asked the boy.

"Come and look! Out at sea. There's a light! Can you see it?"

By this time, Eric had joined Sid at the window. He followed where the old man was pointing.

Outside, it was growing dark. The sea was still raging in the storm. Huge waves were rolling and breaking, and a mist was swirling. So it was hard to make out much detail, but there was definitely a light flashing **on** and **off** at irregular intervals out at sea.

"Is it a ship?" asked Eric.

"It looks too low in the water to be a ship."

"A submarine?"

"Maybe. But what would a British submarine be doing off the coast of Bognor Regis?"

"What if it isn't a British submarine?" said the boy. "What if it's… a Nazi U-boat?"

Just behind him, Eric heard the clinking of crockery.

CHANK! CHUNK!

Gertrude had climbed out of the pram, picked up the teapot and was about to drink from it!

"NOOOO!" cried the boy.

In what felt like slow-motion, Eric leaped through the air…

WHOOSH!

…and snatched the teapot out of the gorilla's hand.

The hot tea was sprayed across the room.

SPLOSH!

It scorched the carpet.

SIZZLE!

The heat of the tea couldn't do that alone. It was clear there was something else in there that was **DEADLY!**

"It's burning the carpet!" said the boy, crouching down to inspect the damage.

"That was **poison** all right," exclaimed Sid. "Thank goodness Gertrude didn't have a drop."

"Let's get it all out of here right now!" said the boy. "Open the window!"

Sid did so, and Eric took everything left on the tray – the milk, the sugar and the biscuits – and dropped them out.

CLUNK! CLINK! CLATTER!

The gorilla looked most disgruntled. She made a loud moaning noise, as if to say, "SPOILSPORT!"

"HHHAAAWWW!"

"Sorry, old girl!" said Sid.

Leaning out of the window, Eric noticed something. At a window along from theirs, another light was flashing. It must be the twins making contact with whoever was out at sea.

"LOOK!

The twins are flashing a
light back!"
Sid put his head out of the
window and observed the pattern of
the flashes.

"It's Morse code," he said.

"Dot dash, dot dash and all that?"

"Exactly. They are spelling out words to each
other in flashes of light."

"Do you know what they are saying?"

"Grab me that postcard and pencil on the desk."

There were a few dog-eared bits of **Seaview Towers** stationery on the writing desk. Eric hurriedly handed them to the old man.

"I learned Morse code during the First World War. That was twenty-five years ago now. Let's hope I can still remember it."

Instantly, Sid began jotting down all the dots and dashes. A short flash of light was a dot, and a long one a dash.

"Oh no! It's all in German!" huffed Sid. "And my German is very rusty!"

"I don't know much beyond '*Heil Hitler*'!" said Eric. The boy turned back to Gertrude, who was standing just behind them at the window. "I don't think Gertrude can speak German either!" he added, stroking the gorilla behind her big furry ears just where she liked it. "Is there anything you can make out, Uncle Sid?"

"T. O. T. E. N."

"*Töten?* What's that mean?"

"I heard the German soldiers shout it when they charged towards our trench. It means 'kill'."

"Kill who?" asked the boy. "Us?"

"Wait!" Sid made some more notes.

"C. H. U. R. C. H. I. L. L."

Together they exclaimed, "Churchill!"

"Töten Churchill," said Sid. **"Kill Churchill!"**

CHAPTER 52

NAZIS IN BOGNOR REGIS

CLASSIFIED

Somehow Sid, Eric and Gertrude had stumbled across a deadly Nazi plot. At a guesthouse. In Bognor Regis.

"This is **big!**" said Sid, having to sit back down to take it all in. "This is **bigger** than big. This is the **biggest**. Kill our prime minister? Without Churchill, the Nazis would be sure to win this blasted war."

"What can we do?" asked the boy.

"We need to get out of here. Pronto. We need to find a telephone. We need to call **Ten Downing Street** and warn them. Call the police. Call the army. Call Bessie. Call anyone we can!"

"Will they believe us?"

"They'd better believe us, or the world will be in even **bigger** trouble than it already is!"

"**Look!**" exclaimed the boy. "More flashes! **Dot. Dot. Dash. Dot.**"

As Eric spoke, Sid scribbled down the letters to form words. After a while, they had a few.

F. L. U. S. S. T. H. E. M. S. E.
B. O. M. B. E.
S. I. E. G.

The pair pondered the list for a moment. Even Gertrude leaned in to take a look, before becoming distracted by a cockroach crawling across the floor.

SCUTTLE! SCUTTLE! SCUTTLE!

She chased it under the bed. It would make a tasty snack, with those biscuits having been thrown out of the window.

"*Fluss?*" said the boy. "What is '*fluss*'?"

"Well, '*Themse*' sounds like 'Thames', so maybe '*fluss*' is 'river'."

"River Thames! There was a huge map downstairs in the library."

"Interesting," mused Sid, stroking his beard. "Very interesting."

"*Bombe!* Well, it's pretty obvious what that means! But what about '*sieg*'?" asked the boy.

"'*Sieg Heil!*' Those Nazis chant it when they give their salute. It means 'Hail victory!'"

"So '*sieg*' means 'victory'?"

"Yes!"

The boy took a deep breath. This was thrilling and terrifying all at once. "So, what we have is 'kill Churchill, River Thames, a bomb and victory'."

Just then the door swung open.

CREAK!

The twins were standing in the doorway, brandishing machine guns.

"So, you didn't drink the tea we prepared for you? What a pity," purred Bertha.

"It would have been such a quick and easy death for you. But, no, you had to choose the hard way," added Helene.

They pointed their guns straight at Sid and Eric.

"PREPARE TO DIE!" said Bertha.

Just then Gertrude looked up from under the bed with a cockroach in her mouth.

CRUNCH!

The twins looked terrified.

"UH! What is that great big monkey doing here?" demanded Bertha.

"She's not a monkey – she's an ape!" exclaimed Eric.

"Great big ape, then!"

"Gertrude is a gorilla we rescued from **LONDON ZOO**!"

"What a shame that she will die too!" remarked Bertha.

The pair cocked their guns, ready to fire.

CLICK! CLICK!

"I wouldn't shoot us if I were you. You need to keep us alive. We know all about your Nazi plot," said Sid.

"You know nothing!" snapped Bertha.

"Less than nothing!" mocked Helene.

Lightning and thunder struck outside.

CRACKLE! BOOM!

"Is that so?" said Sid. "I was in the army in the First World War. I know Morse code."

The twins shared a look of deep concern.

"We've been spying on you for some time," piped up Eric. "That's why we came here to Seaview Towers in the first place!" he lied.

The boy crossed his arms together for emphasis. Gertrude copied his pose and let out a smug sound.

"HUH!"

"I say we kill them," said Helene. "We kill them right now! Starting with the monkey!"

"APE!" exclaimed the boy.

Helene pointed her machine gun at Gertrude. Eric took a step in front of his friend to protect her, and Sid took a step in front of him. Then Gertrude came round the back and stood in front of both of them. It was like a game of musical chairs.

"KEEP STILL!" ordered Bertha, a troubled look on her face. "I need to think!"

"You need to think," taunted Eric, "because you don't know what we know! And that radio downstairs in the living room! Who might we have called on it and told all about who you are plotting to kill?"

"Mr Churchill himself, perhaps?" added Sid.

The twins' faces soured. They snapped at each other in German, talking over each other at lightning speed. Neither Sid nor Eric (nor indeed Gertrude, who looked mightily confused) could make out a word of what they were saying. But Eric knew they had spooked the two.

"YOU ARE COMING WITH US!" barked Bertha. "IN TIME, WE CAN TORTURE YOU AND FIND OUT EXACTLY WHAT YOU KNOW! NOW WALK!"

The pair pointed their machine guns towards the bedroom door. Sid and Eric took one of Gertrude's hands each and led her past the twins, out of the room. However, as soon as they were through the door, Eric slammed it shut in the twins' faces and shouted, "RUN!"

RAT-TAT-TAT!

A hail of bullets ripped through the bedroom door, narrowly missing them.

Our heroes sped down the stairs to the front door. Eric turned the handle, but it wouldn't budge.

"LOCKED!" he exclaimed.

Just then the twins opened the bullet-ridden bedroom door.

CREAK!

They stood on the landing, taking aim at the trio below with their machine guns.

"I have the key!" cried Bertha. "You are TRAPPED!"

"Gertrude!" hissed the boy, miming putting his shoulder up against the door.

The gorilla instantly knew what to do. She nodded her head and charged at the door. Using all her might, she smashed it off its hinges.

BASH!

The door crashed to the ground.

BANG!

The three dashed out as a hail of bullets exploded all around them.

RAT-TAT-TAT!

Holding on to Gertrude's hands, they raced down

the path. A series of police vehicles were speeding to a stop on the road below.

SCREECH!

As the policemen leaped out, Eric spotted that with them were **Sir Frederick Frown, Corporal Batter** and the zoo's deadly vet, **Miss Gnarl.**

"GRRRR!" she growled.

CHAPTER | 53 |

SHOOT THAT GOWILLA!

"Seaview Towers!" announced Frown grandly. "This is the place where the gowilla will be hiding! Just as the pawwot told us!"

"Parker repeats everything!" hissed Sid. "She must have given the game away."

"At least now they are here, everything's going to be all right!" replied the boy.

"At least we won't get killed!" said Sid. "And we can tell them all about the Nazi plot!"

"HELLO!" shouted Eric. "OVER HERE!"

Eric and Sid began frantically waving their hands in the air as they hurried along the path towards them.

They were safe.

Or so they thought.

But they thought wrong!

Just as they were a few paces away, Frown shouted,

"SHOOT THAT GOWILLA!"

"WITH PLEASURE, SIR!" replied Batter as he cocked his rifle and took aim.

BANG! BANG! BANG!

"STOP!" shouted Eric as the bullets whistled over his head, narrowly missing them.

But they didn't stop.

BANG!

BANG! BANG!

Gnarl fired her dart gun.

SCHTUM!

A dart hit the trunk of a tree above our heroes' heads.

T W O N G !

"**Grrrrr!**" growled Gnarl, reloading.

Meanwhile, still holding on to Gertrude's hand, Eric swung her and Sid round.

Now they were running back up the hill towards the guesthouse!

"Why are we going back there?" huffed the breathless old man, struggling to keep up on his tin legs. "They'll kill us too!"

CLINK! CLANK! CLUNK!

"I don't know where else to go!" exclaimed the boy.

Just then, they saw the sinister silhouette of the twins with their machine guns framed in the doorway of **Seaview Towers.**

"Let's head down through the garden!" hissed Sid. "Maybe we can escape across the beach!"

"Good plan!" said Eric.

So they took a sharp turn away from the guesthouse to escape through the overgrown garden.

"I've got a stitch!" moaned the old man, and he leaned on an old stone birdbath. Eric and Gertrude continued for a moment without him, just the other side of some bushes.

Looking back through the foliage, the boy spotted

that Frown, Batter and Gnarl had caught up with Sid. Batter pointed his rifle at the old man.

CLICK!

"Don't shoot!" pleaded Sid.

"Then tell us where the gorilla is!" replied Batter.

"I will, but I need to tell you something."

"What?" demanded Frown.

"We have uncovered a top-secret Nazi plot!"

"In Bognor Wegis?" spluttered Frown.

"Yes. In Bognor Wegis! Oh! Now you've got me doing it!"

"You are a liar, Sidney Pwatt. Now, tell us where the gowilla is wight now!"

"**GRRRR!**" growled Gnarl to add emphasis.

Meanwhile, Eric and Gertrude had tiptoed behind the trio from the zoo.

"Warm!" replied Sid, as if they were playing a game of hide-and-seek. "Warmer. Very warm. Hot! Boiling!"

"What are you on about?" demanded Batter.

"Don't turn round!" said Sid.

Of course, that was exactly what the three did.

On seeing the gorilla so close up, they were startled. Batter fumbled with his rifle, readying it to shoot!

Gertrude grabbed the gun just in time.

"LET GO!" shouted Batter.

But the gorilla wouldn't let go. Instead, she held the rifle with both hands and swung the man round and round by it until he was nothing but a **BLUR!**

RRRRRRRRRRR!

"DON'T LET GO!" shouted Batter.

But this time the gorilla would let go.

WHIZZ!

"HHHHHEEEEEEELLLP!"

Batter went flying through the air and landed with a

SPLOSH! in the pond.

Miss Gnarl then took aim at the gorilla with her dart gun.

But Eric gave her hand a shove as she pulled the trigger. The dart hit Frown in the bottom.

"ARGH!"

he cried in pain, as the dart
knocked him out cold.
He slumped to the ground.

THUD!

"**GRRRR!**" growled Gnarl, as she tried to reload.

Fortunately, the vet wasn't fast enough as Sid snatched
the dart gun from her.

"**GRRRRR!**"

Then with all her might Gertrude lifted up the vet by
her waist and hurled her high into the air.

SWISH!

"**GRURURURURURURURURUR!**"

Gnarl landed in a tall tree.

STONK!

"GRRRRR!"

growled Gnarl. It was far too high for her
to get down without a ladder.

"Hoo! Hoo!" exclaimed Sid.
"That showed them!"

"Don't get cocky! We still need to
make a dash for it!" exclaimed Eric.

CHAPTER | 54 |

BULLETS IN THE BACK

The gang of three hurried down a set of steep stone steps cut into the cliff that led on to the beach.

CLINK! CLANK! CLUNK!

For now, they couldn't hear anyone following them.

The beach was deserted, as well it might be on a dark, stormy winter night such as this.

"I think we lost them!" said Eric, breathless from running.

The boy looked across the rolling waves out to sea. A deep sense of dread crashed over him as he spotted something slowly rise from the water.

At first it was just a long, thin tube. *A periscope!*

Then a flag. The swastika!

Then the metal hull of a submarine reared out of the sea.

"You were right, Eric," muttered a shocked Sid. "It's a Nazi U-boat!"

In times like this, when you are faced with grave danger, there is always one simple option.

RUN AWAY!
RUN AWAY! AS FAST AS YOU CAN!
RUN RUN RUN RUN RUN FASTER
FASTER **FASTER!**

"Let's get out of here!" exclaimed Eric. "FAST!"

"Help me up, lad!" said Sid. "These tin legs of mine have got creaky."

As Eric and Gertrude hauled the old man to his feet, behind them they heard the crunch of feet on the pebbles.

It was the twins, their machine guns pointing right at them.

"Put your hands in the air!" ordered Bertha.

"One move and we will shoot!" commanded Helene.

Eric and Sid shared a look.

"Are we still allowed to put our hands up, though?" asked Sid.

"What?" barked Bertha.

"Does that count as moving?"

"Yes!" snapped Bertha. "Put your hands in the air. One move after that and we will shoot!"

"It could have been clearer!" muttered Sid.

"Don't push your luck, old-timer, or you will find yourself floating face down in the sea with a hail of bullets in your back," replied Bertha.

It was a chilling image, and silenced Sid and Eric in an instant.

"We are going to keep you alive. For now. Until we find out exactly what you know and crucially who you've told about our little plan," continued Bertha.

There was a line of little wooden fishermen's boats where the beach met the road.

"You, boy!" ordered Helene. "You come with me!"

Gertrude sensed fear. These two were spooky at the best of times. She wanted to go with Eric and began following him as he moved off.

"WHOOP!" she hooted.

"Control that monkey or I will put a bullet in its brain!" ordered Bertha.

Sid held the ape back. Eric felt this was not the moment to correct her mistake.

Under Helene's direction, the boy was ordered to heave the rowing boat down to the shore. With machine guns trained on them at such close range, escape was impossible. Our three heroes climbed into the boat, followed by the twins.

"Now row!" barked Bertha.

With Gertrude sitting between them, Sid and Eric rowed the boat out to sea.

It was punishing work, fighting against the waves, but

they made progress. The Nazi U-boat, which was bobbing up and down in the stormy sea, was now lined with what you might describe as a welcoming committee. A number of the submariners were standing to attention on the deck.

At the front was the captain: a handsome man with bright blue eyes and blond hair. He wore a roll-neck sweater and a peaked cap with a badge of an eagle holding a swastika.

On seeing Sid and Eric, he looked surprised. On seeing the gorilla, he burst out laughing.

"*Ein Gorilla?* Ha! Ha! Ha!"

It was clear he was not expecting to see her. Or, indeed, this little boy or old man.

The three prisoners were ordered out of the rowing boat. Sid and Eric looked back to the twins.

"No funny business!" snapped Bertha, brandishing her machine gun.

As soon as the three jumped on to the deck of the submarine, three brutish submariners grabbed them roughly by their arms.

Next, the twins stepped aboard. They shared a Nazi salute with the captain and chanted, "*Heil Hitler!*"

The captain whisked off his cap and bowed. Then he kissed both the twins on their hands, in a show that said he held them in the highest regard. The Brauns blushed at this gentlemanly display.

There was then a long conversation in German between the captain and the twins. From their looks and gestures it was obvious they were discussing the three prisoners. After a final nod from the captain, Sid, Eric and Gertrude were bundled down through the hatch and into the hull of the U-boat.

Soon everyone, including the Braun twins, was inside, and the ladder was pushed back up into position above.

Immediately, Eric felt a curious mixture of fear and excitement. He felt guilty for feeling excited, but he was an eleven-year-old boy on an enemy submarine, and it *was* exciting! Eric was sure to be the only British boy ever to have set foot on a Nazi U-boat.

But would he live to tell the tale?

PART FIVE

THE DARKEST HOUR

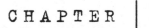

CHAPTER | 55 |

PRISONERS UNDER THE WAVES

The Nazi U-boat was infinitely more cramped on the inside than you could imagine from the outside. It was bustling with submariners attending to the radios, radars, gauges, dials and valves keeping the submarine powering through the sea. Eric, Sid and Gertrude were led along the narrow gangway to the stern (or back) of the U-boat by the three brutish submariners.

The first was short and stout, with a neck that was as wide as his head. The second had a scar on his face that went right across one of his eyes, which was all white. The third was so hefty that he barely fitted down the gangway. He was bald but had a big bushy moustache. This submariner had been put in charge of the gorilla.

Just as Sid and Eric had never been on a submarine before, this was definitely a new experience for Gertrude. Each step of the way, the gorilla wanted to look and explore her new surroundings. She must have been peckish because she kept on trying to **wriggle** out of the submariner's grip and lick every tap, handle and gauge!

"SLURP!"

But the hefty man roughly bustled her along.

"HEE-HAW!" she moaned.

As they made their way through the vessel, the boy noticed that everywhere he looked there were large black cylinders strapped to the hull with rope. There must have been hundreds of them, all emblazoned with a swastika.

"What are all these for?" hissed Eric to Sid. "They don't look like part of the submarine."

"**SILENCE!**" snapped the bald submariner, squeezing on the boy's arms with his sausage fingers to cause pain.

"**OW!**" screamed Eric.

Gertrude wasn't going to let her best friend be treated like this! She tore free of the hefty submariner's grip and bared her fangs, ready to do battle.

"**GRRRRR!**"

The three startled men began barking at each other in German.

"Don't hurt her! Please!" begged Eric.

The submariners fetched a thick rope. When they tried to tie Gertrude up with it, the gorilla fought them off.

"**HOOO!**"

But the submariners were strong and worked fast. In

no time, they had wound the rope round the gorilla so she couldn't move her arms.

"**GRRRR!**" she growled as she tried to wrestle free.

Then they pulled hard on the rope.

"**HEEEEE!**" yelped the gorilla in pain.

The boy ran at the submariners.

"Eric, no!" cried Sid. "They'll kill us!"

The bald man picked up the boy by the scruff of his neck and carried him down the gangway.

Next, the three prisoners were bustled into a cramped cabin, before being pushed down on to the floor. Their hands were held behind their backs as they were chained to a metal pipe.

CLANK! CLANK! CLANK!

Gertrude was chained in the middle, with Sid and Eric on either side.

"**WHOOP! WHOOP!**" whooped the gorilla. It was agony for all of them.

"It'll be all right, Gertrude!" said the boy. "We'll get out of here. I don't know how, but we will."

"We can't let these blighters win!" agreed Sid.

The three brutish submariners admired their handiwork.

They chuckled to themselves, before leaving the cabin, locking the door behind them.

"HA! HA! HA!"

It looked as if they were in the captain's private quarters. There was a narrow bed, a small but elegant desk and chair, a clock on the wall and a Nazi flag. In pride of place on the shelf was a silver-framed photograph of the captain being awarded an Iron Cross First Class, one of the highest medals in the German military, by Adolf Hitler himself.

There were also maps and charts pinned around the walls, showing the route of the U-boat's top-secret mission. It was travelling along the English south coast now, before making its way up the Thames Estuary and finally arriving in London. This map was marked in the exact same place as the map Eric had spotted in **Seaview Towers.**

"Parlament" had been scribbled next to a spot circled in red. You didn't need to be a genius to translate it.

"That must be their target," guessed Eric. "The Houses of Parliament!"

"Blow up that and it's not just goodbye, Churchill, but it's goodbye, entire government too!" said Sid.

"Britain would be brought to its knees. Blasted bad luck we didn't get to a telephone to warn anyone!"

"There still must be something we can do to stop them."

Gertrude was leaning her head to one side, clearly trying to follow the conversation. She was struggling to keep up but nodding away with the pair.

Suddenly there was the sound of voices outside.

"**Shush!**" shushed Sid. "Let's listen."

The gorilla angled one of her big furry ears in the direction of the door.

Outside, the captain was having an argument in German with the twins.

"That captain's not happy about us upsetting their plans. Not happy one bit," was Sid's verdict.

After a while, the door was unlocked.

CLICK!

The captain entered his cabin, sporting a sinister smile.

"Good evening," he said, speaking perfect English. "Welcome aboard my U-boat. I am Captain Speer. Well, well, well, what an unlikely trio of spies we have. An old man, a little boy and a monkey!"

"Ape!" corrected Eric. He couldn't help himself.

Gertrude nodded her head.

"I stand corrected! Ape! The question is," continued the captain, crouching down so he was at head height with them, "who have you told about our top-secret mission?"

Then he left a long, uncomfortable silence hanging in the air. It was extremely tempting to fill it, but Sid said nothing, and Eric followed his lead. Gertrude, however, had other ideas. She blew a big, wet raspberry right in the captain's face.

"PFFFFFFT!"

Sid and Eric burst out laughing.

"HA! HA! HA!"

Speer smiled, though not in a way that suggested he found it funny.

"The famous British sense of humour! Have a good laugh, my friends. In a matter of hours, your beloved prime minister, Mr Winston Churchill, will be dead."

"You won't succeed!" exclaimed Eric.

"Oh yes we will. My mission has been personally supervised by the Führer himself. Hitler knows that with Churchill dead Britain will be like a chicken with its head chopped off. Running around in a fury for a few moments, before it simply keels over and dies. Bwark! Bwark! Bwark!"

Speer's impersonation of a headless chicken was surprisingly good.

"And that will be the perfect moment to strike! The Nazi invasion of Britain will finally begin! And you will all kneel before the Führer!"

"I have already warned **Ten Downing Street** all about this mission," lied Eric.

"Have you now?"

"They know that a Nazi U-boat is heading to the Houses of Parliament and that Churchill is the target!"

Sid and Gertrude turned their heads to look at Eric, clearly praying that the boy knew what he was doing!

CHAPTER | 56

THE BIGGEST BOMB IN THE WORLD

"Interesting! Very interesting!" purred Speer. "And how did a little boy like you contact **Ten Downing Street** exactly? Sent a postcard? Ha! Ha!"

"No. I radioed them on the wireless at Seaview Towers!" replied Eric, thinking fast.

Sid and Gertrude nodded along with Eric as Speer's face darkened with worry. "I would be most surprised if a boy like you was able to work a complex piece of equipment like that."

"It was easy! I do science at school and I actually listen in that lesson," said Eric, lying again. He didn't listen in any lessons.

"You are lying!" snapped Speer.

"How can you be sure, Captain Speer?" said Sid. "That's why you and the twins are keeping us alive, isn't it?"

"That is true, old-timer! Still, the wireless was used

only for listening, not for speaking. It was built especially for our Nazi spies in Britain, Bertha and Helene Braun. With the radio, they could listen in to British secret-service communications. It had to be on British soil as the signals could not be picked up in Germany, or under the sea, as we are now."

"So that's how you found out where Churchill would be?" said the boy.

"Exactly right, child. The madames are genius code breakers. They discovered that your prime minister is having a top-secret conference with all the members of his government at midnight tonight. The heads of the British army, navy and air force will also be in attendance. We will wipe them all out in one fell swoop!"

Eric, Sid and Gertrude gulped.

"GULP!"

The plan was even more dastardly than they'd thought.

"Who do you think you are, trying to kill Churchill?" demanded Sid.

"I think – in fact, I know – that I am the most decorated captain in the Nazi German navy. Just at Dunkirk alone, I torpedoed three of your British warships."

These words startled Eric. His father was killed when the boat on which he was fleeing France, HMS *Grafton*, was torpedoed. The boy could feel a fury raging inside him. "Not HMS *Grafton*?" he demanded.

Captain Speer smiled to himself at the memory. "Yes, the biggest of them all, the *Grafton*."

"MURDERER!" shouted Eric, shaking with anger. "My dad was on that boat."

"WHOOP!" whooped Gertrude, trying to wriggle out of the rope.

"Was he indeed?" smirked Speer. "One of so many souls who died on that vessel. That is war."

Eric broke down in tears at the memory of losing his dad. It was all coming back to him now. The look on Mum's face when he had returned home from school; without a word being said, he'd known instantly that the worst had happened. He'd had nightmares imagining his father's final moments.

"I wish I could hold you right now," said Sid, shifting a little in his chains as the boy sobbed.

"HOOOOOO!" agreed Gertrude.

She knew the boy was hurting, even if she didn't

know why. The gorilla nuzzled her big head to the boy's face, wiping away his tears with her fur.

"Thank you, Uncle Sid. Thank you, Gertrude," whispered the boy.

She moaned quietly, trying to say something, something soothing.

"HHHMMM!"

Eric couldn't speak gorilla, but he knew what she meant.

"I will take great pleasure in killing you just as I took great pleasure in killing your father!" purred Speer.

Eric tried to wrestle out of the chains to give this wicked man a biff on the nose, but it was no use.

"You monster!" cried the boy. **"That's not just war – that's pure evil!"**

Gertrude tried to break free too. It was impossible.

KERCHANG!

Instead she growled at the man, baring her teeth.

"GRRR!"

Speer took a step backwards. Gertrude could be a fearsome beast when she wanted to be.

"Control that walking fur coat of yours or I will shoot it this instant!" ordered Speer, reaching for the pistol in his holster.

"I hate to tell you this, Captain Speer, but your whole plan is doomed to fail!" spat Sid. "There is no way a torpedo is going to be able to destroy the whole of the Houses of Parliament!"

"Torpedo?" laughed the captain. "We are not going to fire a torpedo!"

Sid and Eric were mystified. Even Gertrude looked confused.

"Then how are you going to kill Churchill?" asked the old man.

"This entire U-boat is packed with explosives. Here, here, here," he said, indicating the black cylinders strapped to the walls. "There are hundreds of these packed all around the boat. Each one of them as powerful as a torpedo. When this U-boat hits the Houses of Parliament, **KABOOM!** We will destroy the entire building in the blink of an eye!"

Sid and Eric looked at each other, shocked. Gertrude looked shocked too, even though she didn't know what she was shocked about.

"But… but… but… if the whole submarine is a bomb, then how will you survive?" spluttered the boy.

"I won't. Myself, the entire crew and the twins have all signed up for what will be our final mission."

"Final mission?" repeated Eric, incredulous.

"Yes! We will all die for the glory of the Führer! We will be celebrated as Nazi heroes until the end of time!"

"But what about us?" asked Eric, rather pitifully.

"You will, of course, be killed too," purred Captain Speer. "But all in good time. Patience, as you British say, is a virtue."

With that, he politely tipped his captain's cap and

disappeared

through

the door.

CHAPTER 57

TICKLISH

Time passed, but Eric kept checking the clock on the wall in the captain's cabin. It was now a quarter to twelve.

 Just fifteen minutes until midnight when the U-boat and everyone in it was going to destroy the Houses of Parliament.

KABOOM!

Winston Churchill, everyone in the British government and all three heads of the armed forces would be killed instantly. The Nazis would then be free to invade Britain just as they'd marched into so much of Europe.

"Well, who'd have thought that by rescuing Gertrude from the zoo that we'd end up here?" said Sid.

"It's lucky we did!" replied Eric.

"Lucky? How?"

"We've got a chance to be heroes."

"You're right. That's all I've ever wanted," said the

old man, tears budding in his eyes. "My legs were taken from me all those years ago on my very first day on the battlefields of France. I was sent straight back to Blighty. Now I've got one last chance to finally be a hero."

"This is it! We can do it, Uncle Sid! Me and you and, of course, Gertrude here can save Churchill."

The gorilla nodded. Gertrude wasn't sure exactly what she was nodding for, but she was always up for adventure.

"How can we?" asked Sid.

"I don't know yet. I'm only eleven. But, first things first, we need to get out of these chains," said the boy, rattling away at them with little effect.

KERCHANG!

"They're impossible for us to break through," added Sid as he tried too.

KERCHANG!

"For us, yes, but maybe not for Gertrude. She is so strong that she broke through her cage, remember?"

This stopped Sid in his tracks. The boy had a point.

"But how are we going to tell Gertrude to break through the chains? I don't speak gorilla, and neither do you."

"She'll understand if we mime," suggested Eric.

"She might."

Both then performed their best pantomime of the chains being torn apart, but sadly Gertrude merely shook her head and frowned as if they were both bananas.

"I've got an idea!" exclaimed the boy. "If we tickle her, she might just **wriggle** enough, and break this pipe! Then we'd be free!"

With his head, Eric nodded to the pipe running along the floor. It was a thick steel pipe, one of hundreds that snaked along the length of the U-boat.

"It's worth a try!" agreed Sid.

"Let's take off our shoes."

"You what?"

"We'll have to use our toes to tickle."

"I don't have any toes!"

"Tin toes! Just try!"

The pair kicked off their shoes. Next, with great difficulty, they manoeuvred themselves into positions where their feet were at the same level as Gertrude's armpits.

For most people, armpits are their most ticklish spot, but when they both tickled the gorilla there she hardly reacted at all.

TICKLE! TICKLE! TICKLE!

It was like Gertrude was experiencing a pleasant scratch, rather than something that was going to make her squirm. She smiled to herself and closed her eyes.

"She's not ticklish under her armpits!" cursed the boy. "Let's try under her chin!"

Once again, the pair contorted themselves into new positions where now their feet would be level with the gorilla's chin.

"It's not easy at my age!" complained Sid as his bottom found itself under Eric's nose.

"Don't make any sudden movements!" snapped the boy, fearing the worst.

Now they tickled the gorilla under her chin with their feet.

TICKLE! TICKLE! TICKLE!

All Gertrude did this time was yawn.

"YAWN!"

"Fiddlesticks!" cursed the boy. "Where on earth is Gertrude ticklish?"

If only they'd had this handy guide:

WHERE TO TICKLE A GORILLA:

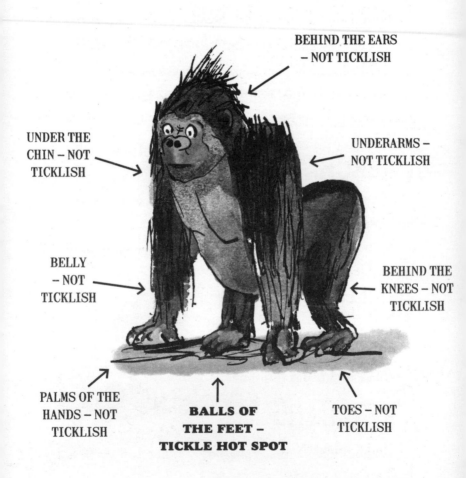

BEHIND THE EARS
– NOT TICKLISH

UNDER THE
CHIN – NOT
TICKLISH

UNDERARMS –
NOT TICKLISH

BELLY
– NOT
TICKLISH

BEHIND THE
KNEES – NOT
TICKLISH

PALMS OF THE
HANDS – NOT
TICKLISH

**BALLS OF
THE FEET –
TICKLE HOT SPOT**

TOES – NOT
TICKLISH

This gorilla-tickling experiment went on for quite a while until the pair finally hit **GOLD!**

The balls of the feet!

Sid and Eric ended up upside down doing it.

TICKLE! TICKLE! TICKLE!

Immediately, the gorilla was whooping with laughter.

"HEE! HEE! HEE!"

Not just that, she was now rocking and wriggling with such force that the metal chain they were all attached to yanked against the pipe.

KERCHANG!

"Keep going, Gertrude!" said Eric.

"You can do it, old girl!" egged on Sid.

With some difficulty, the pair kept tickling the underside of Gertrude's huge hairy feet.

TICKLE! TICKLE! TICKLE!

The more they tickled, the more she convulsed.

TICKLE! TICKLE! TICKLE!

"HEE! HEE! HEE!"

KERCHANG! KERCHANG! KERCHANG!

Until eventually...

SNAP!

The pipe broke in two, spraying sparks of electricity into the cabin.

FIZZLE! FAZZLE! FOZZLE!

With the pipe snapped, Sid and Eric could free themselves too and scrambled to their feet.

"Yes!" exclaimed the boy.

"The boys are back in business!" agreed Sid.

They both hugged Gertrude tight.

With her ginger eyes, the gorilla indicated the thick rope that was still tied round her.

"Oh yes, of course!" said Eric.

As fast as they could, he and Sid unwrapped her like a Christmas present.

"There you go, Gertrude! And so sorry for tickling you!" said the boy. "But it was the only way."

The sparks from the electric cables in the pipe were now exploding into the cabin.

FIZZLE! FAZZLE! FOZZLE!

It was like a fireworks display!

WHIZZ! SNAPPLE! BANG!

Sparks flew higher and higher until the Nazi flag caught alight.

WHOOMPH!

"Best thing for it!" remarked Sid.

However, smoke from the burning flag must have set off an alarm, as the U-boat throbbed with the sound of a bell.

DDDRRRIIINNNGGG!

"We need to get out of here!" said Eric.

At that moment, the cabin door swung open. The Braun twins stood in the doorway, sporting swastika armbands and wielding their machine guns. On seeing the three had escaped from their chains, Bertha barked, "We've had quite enough of you three ruining our plans!"

Helene added,
"PREPARE TO DIE!"

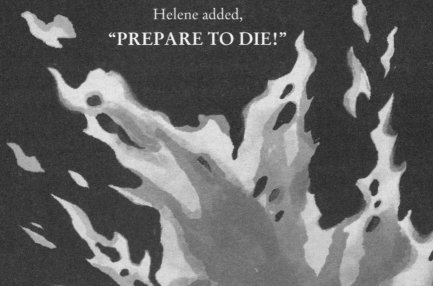

CHAPTER | 58 |

BOTTOM ON FIRE

"You well know if you fire those machine guns in here we're all dead," shouted Sid.

The twins' faces soured, if indeed they could sour any more as they were already incredibly sour. They knew the old man was right. The pair spun their machine guns round in their hands…

WHIZZ!

…so they could use the butts as weapons. They weren't highly prized Nazi spies for nothing! The ladies surged forward, ready to strike Eric and Sid.

"HOO!"

But Gertrude leaped in the way to protect them. As she did so, the gorilla grabbed both Braun twins' heads in her big, hairy hands.

"*NEIN!*" shouted Bertha and Helene together.

Like cracking a coconut, the gorilla clonked their

heads together. CLONK!

In an instant, the pair fell to the floor, their arms and legs splayed, forming the shapes of swastikas.

DONK! DONK!

"Nazis to the end," remarked Sid, before turning to Gertrude. "Excellent work, old girl!"

The gorilla looked pleased with herself as she smiled broadly and beat her chest.

BOOM! BOOM! BOOM!

But the celebration was short-lived – the fire in the captain's cabin had now spread to his bed!

WHOOMPH!

It went up in flames.

Gertrude began crying in fear. "WHOOP! WHOOP!"

"What are we going to do?" asked Eric.

"We need to sink this submarine before it hits the Houses of Parliament."

Eric looked at the clock on the wall. It was now just five minutes to midnight. Captain Speer was a meticulous character. He was sure to be exact in his timing and strike the Houses of Parliament dead on midnight.

"How are we going to do that?" asked Eric.

"We'll scuttle it!"

"What?"

"Flood it! Open all the hatches, let the water rush in. Let it plunge to the bottom of the Thames!"

"How will we get out alive?" asked the boy.

"There's very little chance of that, I'm afraid. Let me try to get you and Gertrude out of here, and then this U-boat can go down with me."

"No, Uncle Sid!" said the boy. "I'm staying to help you! I've lost my mum, my dad and my granny. I can't lose you too!"

The gorilla nodded her head.

"LOOK!" shouted Eric, pointing out of the cabin doorway to the long gangway.

Submariners were charging towards them, armed with anything they could lay their hands on. Spanners. Wrenches. Hammers.

A flame from the bed licked Gertrude's backside.

WHOOMPH!

Feeling that her furry bottom was on fire, she yelped.

"WHOOOOO!"

The gorilla charged out of the cabin, away from the

flames, down the gangway. One by one, she hurled the submariners out of her way.

"ARGH!"

DOINK!

None of them stood a chance against a fearsome beast with its bottom on fire!

"URGH!"

DOINK!

Gertrude picked them up and flung them against the side of the submarine.

"AAHH!"

DOINK!

However, she saved something special for her main tormentor. The bald submariner with the bushy moustache was in for a treat! Gertrude smirked on seeing him. With both hands, she grabbed him by his moustache.

"*NEIN! NEIN!*" he cried.

The gorilla then swung the man round and round by his moustache.

"ARGH!" he cried.

WHOOSH! WHOOSH! WHOOSH!

Then she let go!

The flying submariner took out some others who were running to his defence. They were knocked over like skittles!

BONK! BONK! BONK!

All Eric and Sid had to do was step over the submariners, all of whom were knocked out cold on the gangway floor. Catching up with the gorilla, the three ran to the control room.

"This way!" said Sid, leading them.

The control room was buzzing with activity.

"*Parlamentsgebäude in Reichweite, Kapitän!*" shouted a submariner as he looked through the periscope.

"Parliament in range!" translated Sid to Eric and Gertrude. "We're in the middle of London!

We're about to hit!"

CHAPTER 59

CHOMP!

The captain himself was at the steering wheel of his U-boat.

"*Eine Minute bis es explodiert!*" he barked to his crew.

"One minute to explosion!" translated Sid.

Upon seeing the three, the captain shouted over the noise of the fire bell ringing, "You cannot stop us now!"

"Eric! The ladder!" shouted Sid. "Climb up and open the hatch!"

The boy ran to the bottom of the ladder, but it had been pushed upwards to be stored. It could only be reached by a grown-up, not a rather short eleven-year-old boy. "I can't reach!"

Sid charged over to where the boy was standing, but Speer thumped the old man on the back of the head with the butt of his pistol, and he fell to the ground.

424

THUMP!

"UNCLE SID!" shouted the boy.

The gorilla bared her fangs and snarled at the captain.

"ROAR!"

"Don't worry about me!" called the old man from the floor. "Open that hatch!"

"Gertrude!" shouted Eric.

"Over here! I need your help!"

The gorilla leaped across to the boy.

THUMP!

Eric jumped on her back, and Gertrude leaped up towards the hatch.

BOING!

The boy's hands grabbed the bottom of the ladder, and it slid down to the floor.

CLANK!

"Thanks, Gertrude!" he said, climbing off the gorilla's back to scale the ladder.

Then Gertrude jumped down to tend to Sid as Eric tried to open the hatch.

"STOP THAT BOY!" shouted Speer, but his crew were too scared to try to pass this ginormous ape.

"COWARDS!" he screamed, before abandoning his steering wheel. The submarine immediately felt as if it were lurching off course.

CREAK!

The captain raced over and grabbed hold of the boy's legs.

"NOT SO FAST!" cried Speer, trying to yank the boy down. He'd very nearly done it, but Gertrude had now helped Sid up to his feet, and the old man rushed over to tackle Speer.

"See if he's ticklish, Uncle Sid!" shouted Eric.

"I am the most highly decorated captain of the entire U-boat fleet!" protested Speer. "I am not ticklish anywhere!"

"Everyone's ticklish somewhere!" said the boy.

Immediately, Sid went to work, tickling the man's ankles, then behind his knees, but there was no reaction.

If only Sid had had this handy guide:

WHERE TO TICKLE A NAZI U-BOAT CAPTAIN:

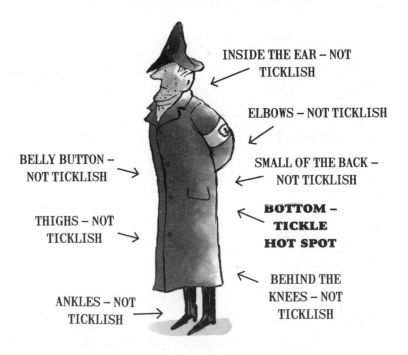

INSIDE THE EAR – NOT TICKLISH

ELBOWS – NOT TICKLISH

BELLY BUTTON – NOT TICKLISH

SMALL OF THE BACK – NOT TICKLISH

THIGHS – NOT TICKLISH

BOTTOM – TICKLE HOT SPOT

ANKLES – NOT TICKLISH

BEHIND THE KNEES – NOT TICKLISH

If Sid had been in possession of such a guide, he would have known exactly where to tickle Captain Speer. As it was, he tried lots of places to no effect whatsoever, so he called for help.

"GERTRUDE!" he cried.

The gorilla lunged at the submariners to startle them...

"GRRRR!"

...before leaping over to the ladder.

Somehow, the animal knew exactly what to do.

Go straight for the bottom!

Gertrude tickled Speer there for a moment...

TICKLE! TICKLE! TICKLE!

"OH! HA! HA! PLEASE! NO!"

Then she went in for the kill. The gorilla bared her fangs and sank them right into the captain's buttocks.

CHOMP!

"OOOWWW!" screamed Speer.

The captain immediately tumbled down on top of Gertrude and Sid.

"I've nearly done it!" called Eric. "Are you sure I should open this?"

"Scuttling the submarine is our only hope of saving Churchill!" shouted Sid.

So the boy took a deep breath and spun the final lock on the hatch. With all his might, he pushed the hatch against the weight of the River Thames above. But he just couldn't do it. It was far too heavy.

"GERTRUDE!" he called down.

The ape leaped up on to the ladder. The boy mimed what he was trying to do, and Gertrude nodded her head.

"You are not going to like it, Gertrude. I know you hate water!" said the boy.

The gorilla shrugged. Together they pushed the hatch on the top of the U-boat and let the filthy black water flood in.

SPLOOOSH!

The force of the water washed them both down into the hull.

THUD!

It swept all those in the U-boat off their feet.

SPLOOOSH!

Gertrude screamed, "WHOOP! WHOOP!"

Gorillas can't swim and the poor creature was up to her waist in water.

"HOLD ON, OLD GIRL!" cried Sid. He grabbed a mop to reach the gorilla. However, while yanking the mop from the catch on the wall, he'd managed to whack the handle on to his forehead.

CLUNK!

Chomp!

The unlucky old soldier knocked himself out cold.

Captain Speer held on to the steering wheel as the water roared in. Struggling against the flood that was drowning him and his U-boat, he reached for a key that was on a chain round his neck, before plunging it into a lock on the control panel.

As he did so, a large button on the panel lit up red and a **buzzing** sound filled the cabin.

BUZZZ!

"I press this big red button and **KABOOM!**" announced Speer. **"We all die together!"**

CHAPTER **60**

BIG RED BUTTON

Despite having had so many brushes with death, Eric's will to live was strong. He waded through the flooded submarine before hurling himself at the captain, sweeping him off his feet.

DOOF!

Speer fought back, kicking his legs and wriggling free.

"URGH!"

Now his finger was just out of reach of the big red button.

Still the **dark, filthy** Thames water flooded in. The poor gorilla was now up to her neck in it and flailing around in desperation.

"WOOOH!"

SPLOSH!

More terror was to come. The weight of the water caused the U-boat to upend, throwing Captain Speer off his station. The submarine descended to the riverbed.

CREAK!

Eric desperately swam up to the air pocket to have a gasp.

"GASP!"

Sid was floating face down in the water, and Eric feared the worst. Meanwhile, the gorilla's head was slipping into the depths.

BLUB! BLUB! BLUB!

Eric turned Sid over so he could breathe. Then he grabbed the gorilla.

"GERTRUDE! HOLD ON!"

The terrified animal just managed to grasp on to the boy's back.

Meanwhile, Speer yanked an underwater breathing device off the wall and placed it over his face. The man seemed hellbent on pressing the red self-destruct button and causing as much death and devastation as he possibly could.

"For the glory of the Führer!" he shouted, before diving down below.

"Oh no!" muttered Eric. "Gertrude! Hold on to Sid! I'm going after him!"

The boy managed to unhook the gorilla's arms from round his chest and place them over the old man, before diving down into the depths after Speer.

SPLOSH!

The water was so dirty it was hard to see anything other than a blur, but Eric could just make out the large grey air tank on the captain's back. Just as Speer reached **the red button**, the boy grabbed hold of his tank. A vicious struggle began, causing them both to float back up to the stern of the submarine, which now only had a tiny pocket of air at the top.

GASP!

The submariners were swimming past, desperate to escape the sinking U-boat.

"RATS!" exclaimed Speer. "FILTHY COWARDLY RATS, ALL OF YOU! I WILL DESTROY YOU! I WILL DESTROY YOU ALL!"

Using his superior strength, the captain wrestled the air tank from Eric before striking him across the face with it.

BASH!

"ARGH!"

Eric was knocked out.

All was black.

All was silent.

A WATERY GRAVE

The next thing Eric knew, a big rough tongue was licking his face.

"GERTRUDE!" he exclaimed, waking up with a start.

The gorilla held on to Sid with one hand and put the other on her heart to tell the boy how much she loved him.

Eric smiled and did the same.

"Where's the captain?" asked the boy, seeing that the air tank was floating by his side.

The gorilla cocked her head, trying to understand.

Thinking fast, the boy mimed the captain's peaked cap.

Gertrude pointed downwards.

No! thought Eric. *Speer is going to push that red button and we're all going to die!*

BASH!

The U-boat lurched violently as the bow struck the riverbed.

CRANK!

Eric grabbed on to the air tank. Could it somehow be used to propel them all the way up to the surface of the Thames?

There was no way a gorilla could swim it.

Sid was still knocked out cold and Eric couldn't leave him or Gertrude to a watery grave.

The boy heaved the old man into place astride the air tank. Then he mimed for Gertrude to hold on to Sid. Eric then climbed on to the back of the tank.

"LET'S GET OUT OF HERE!"

said the boy, pointing the tank towards the hatch of the U-boat.

Just as he was about to turn the nozzle to let the air shoot out,

DISASTER STRUCK!

The Braun twins had swum up through the U-boat.

"We all die together!" sputtered Bertha.

"For the love of the Führer!" added Helene.

Each sister grabbed hold of one of Sid's ankles to stop them from escaping. There was no time to fight them off, so Eric spun the nozzle...

SPLURT!

Sid's false legs came off in their hands.

PLOP! PLOP!

Those old tin legs of his had come in handy, after all!

As the twins were left behind in the U-boat, clutching on to Sid's legs, shouting...

"*NEIN!*"

...our three heroes shot through the hatch.

SWOOSH!

CHAPTER 62

TIDAL WAVE

It was a long way from the riverbed to the surface of the Thames. The water was black, and it was midnight. Eric couldn't see a thing, but made sure he held tightly to Sid and Gertrude the whole time.

Eventually, they reached the surface.

SPLOOOSH!

"GASP!" gasped the boy as he took in a huge gulp of air. **They were alive!**

Blinking, Eric could see the Houses of Parliament.

Big Ben chimed midnight.

BONG! BONG! BONG! BONG! BONG! BONG! BONG! BONG! BONG! BONG! BONG! BONG!

There on a terrace, the boy spotted the unmistakable figure of Winston Churchill! The old round man was flanked by three men in uniform, who had to be the chiefs of the army, navy and air force. Behind them were assembled notable looking gentlemen and ladies. The complete British government.

All were pointing and staring at the most peculiar trio bouncing along the river on an air tank.

"TAKE COVER!" shouted the boy. "THERE IS A NAZI U-BOAT DOWN THERE THAT IS GOING TO EXPLODE!"

Churchill was hastily ushered back inside, followed by all the others.

Then...

KABOOM!

Speer must have reached that big red button, as a mountain of water blasted into the air.

WHOOSH!

The Houses of Parliament were drenched. It was as if an entire year's rain fell in a single second.

SPLOSH!

The explosion deep in the depths of the Thames created a monstrous tidal wave. It crashed across Westminster Bridge, nearly sweeping off the late-night buses and taxis that were crossing.

WHOOSH!

Eric turned round and looked in horror as he saw the wave, which was as tall as an elephant, chasing them.

WHOOSH!

The boy spun the valve to make the air tank go faster.

SPIN!

But it was already bouncing along the surface of the water like a torpedo.

ZOOM!

Still the wave kept coming.

WHOOSH!

"GERTRUDE!" shouted Eric. "STAND UP! WE'RE GONNA HAVE TO SURF!"

Keeping his balance, the boy stood up on the air tank.

Once there he mimed for the gorilla to follow. With all her strength she heaved up a legless and still knocked-out Sid. Balancing as best they could, they rode the

humongous wave all the way

down the River Thames.

WHOOSH!

The three passed under Blackfriars Bridge, then Southwark Bridge and London Bridge. The wave eventually slowed down to a stop as they approached Tower Bridge. The three heroes found themselves bobbing around in the freezing water, clinging on to each other to stay alive.

Eric spotted a ladder on the side of Tower Bridge that reached all the way down to the river. Holding tightly to Gertrude and Sid, he kicked his legs as hard as he could to reach it.

"THIS WAY!" he shouted.

Gertrude was first to reach the bottom of the ladder. The boy pushed Sid on to her back and wrapped his arms round her. The gorilla knew what to do and clung on to the man's hands under her chin. She made light work of the ladder, leaping up it with terrific speed. Eric followed on behind, as tired as it was possible to be without actually being asleep.

As the boy clambered up the last step and heaved himself on to the bridge, he saw two pairs of big black boots. Looking up, he saw that these boots belonged to two policemen. Both of them had their mouths open, stunned to see a soaking-wet gorilla standing on Tower Bridge with a legless man on its back.

"Lovely night for a swim!" joked the boy. The policemen didn't crack a smile.

Gertrude gently laid Sid down on the ground. The gorilla patted the man, to try to wake him up.

"HOO!"

"Uncle Sid? Uncle Sid?" said the boy, joining in.

"WAKE UP!"

But there were no signs of life.

"WAH!" wailed the gorilla, devastated to have lost her friend.

"Shall we call an ambulance?" asked one of the policemen.

"I think it's too late!" spluttered Eric, choking back tears.

At the cinema, the boy had seen the on-screen heroes close the eyes of their comrades who had died. So he ran his fingers over the old man's eyelids.

"Get your dirty fingers out of my eyes!" protested Sid.

"You're alive!" exclaimed Eric.

Gertrude let out an excited whoop: "WHOOP!"

They both held on tightly to the old man.

"Did I miss anything?" asked Sid.

"Nothing much!" smiled the boy.

"On no! I lost my chance to be a hero!"

"No, you didn't, Uncle Sid. Far from it!" lied Eric. "Don't you remember?"

"Remember what?"

"You took on the captain of the U-boat single-handed."

"I did?"

"Yes, and you fought off the Braun twins."

"Oh my!"

"Uncle Sid, you, and you alone, saved Churchill. **You are a hero!"**

"I am?" spluttered Sid.

"Yes!" fibbed the boy.

"WOOHOO!" rejoiced the old man. "I AM A HERO! DID YOU HEAR THAT, OLD GIRL? YOUR LITTLE OLD ZOOKEEPER! A HERO!"

"HUMMM!" murmured the gorilla, not so convinced.

"We'd better take you to the police station," announced one of the policemen. "Get you warmed up!"

"Yes," agreed the boy.

"We've got quite a tale to tell."

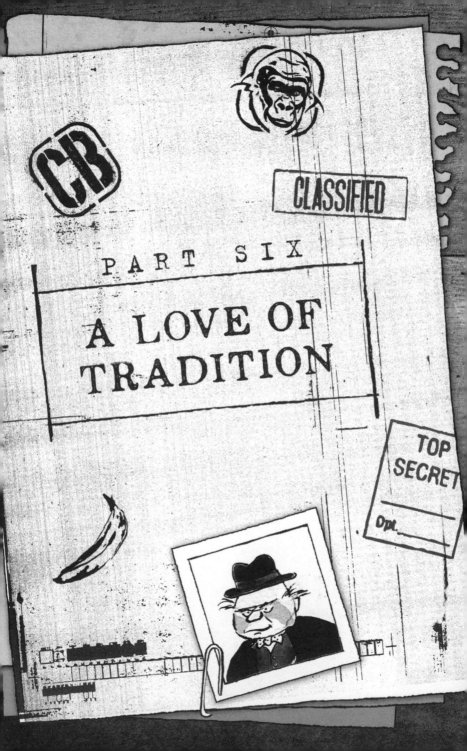

CHAPTER | 63

THE MOST FAMOUS ADDRESS IN THE WORLD

After a change of clothes, a thorough interrogation and some much-needed tea and biscuits, members of the **SECRET INTELLIGENCE SERVICE** (MI6) swooped into the police station. Although the whole idea of the **SECRET INTELLIGENCE SERVICE** was that they were secret, the fact that they all wore trilby hats and mackintosh coats with the collars turned up made them a dead giveaway.

"We are taking over from now on," barked one, holding up an official-looking identity card.

There were more questions, more tea and more biscuits. Then, the next thing the three knew, they were in the back of a wide black car being driven through the streets of London in a convoy at dawn. Low winter light was streaming between the buildings. The city was only just waking up, and Londoners would have had no clue about the incredible drama of last night. Most would have been asleep when a Nazi U-boat very nearly killed the prime minister and ended up exploding in the depths of the Thames.

"Where are we going, please?" asked Eric, who was squashed between Gertrude and a still legless Sid on the bank of back seats.

But the secret servicemen said nothing, and just kept staring forward as if they hadn't even heard the question. Even a version of the popular hit *"We'll Meet Again"*, played purely by Gertrude, Eric and Sid blowing raspberries, failed to bring a smile to their faces.

"PFFT! PFFT! PFFT! PFFT!"

Eventually, Eric realised that the convoy was speeding through Whitehall. They passed the Cenotaph, the war memorial to those who had died in the First World War. Then the car took a sharp turn and came to a stop outside the most famous address in the world.

10 Downing Street.

It had been home to British prime ministers for more than two hundred years. The door of the car was opened, a wheelchair was trundled into place for Sid and the three were ushered inside by a butler.

This was by far the most **magnificent** home in which Eric had ever set foot: the sweeping wooden staircase, the scarlet rugs, the marble floor. They were taken into an office with a huge fireplace and an imposing wooden desk.

The butler asked them to, "Please take a seat."

"I already have!" chirped Sid as he was, indeed, sitting in his wheelchair. Just as with the security servicemen, this failed to amuse the butler, who left the room. They waited in silence for a few moments, trying to stop Gertrude from eating the telephone that was crouching on the desk. After a short while, the door opened, and one of the most famous people in the world stood in the doorway. A short, round man in his sixties, wearing a charcoal three-piece suit with a white shirt and a spotty bow tie, shuffled in.

"Your Majesty!" said Eric, instantly realising he'd got it wrong.

"Not quite yet!" chuckled Churchill.

CHAPTER 64

CLASSIFIED

BADLY BEHAVED
GUESTS

The boy stood up as he might if the headmaster came into the classroom.

"Please, please, no standing on ceremony, thank you," said Churchill.

"Thank goodness for that," said Sid. "Because I can't! A pleasure to meet you, sir!"

"The pleasure is all mine! And who, may I ask, is this rather delightful young lady?" asked the prime minister.

It was a reasonable question as it wasn't every day that he had a gorilla sitting in his office.

"Oh, this is Gertrude, prime minister!" began Eric. "We stole her—"

"RESCUED!" corrected Sid.

"Rescued her from **LONDON ZOO**."

"And from what I saw from the terrace of the Houses of Parliament last night, she helped save me, the heads of the armed forces and the entire British government from certain death!"

"That's right, sir," replied Eric.

"Let's not give Gertrude all the credit, though," began Sid, "as I did my fair share!"

"More than your fair share," agreed the boy.

"**GRRRR!**" growled the gorilla, in strong disagreement.

"So tell me more about this dreadful Nazi plot."

Eric told Winston Churchill the whole story from start to finish. How they'd rescued Gertrude from **LONDON ZOO** with a barrage balloon. How they'd gone on the run from **Frown, Batter and Gnarl**, before escaping to Bognor Regis where they met the evil **Braun twins.** How the Nazi U-boat they were bundled on to was, in fact, a giant bomb! Gertrude helped with the storytelling by acting out some of the scenes. And, of course, Eric kept Sid centre-stage in the story throughout.

Churchill followed this tale of derring-do with great interest.

"Those dastardly Nazis! There is no end to their wretched villainy!" he concluded, opening a box on his desk. "Cigar?"

"I may take one for later if that's all right, sir," said Sid, slipping one in his breast pocket.

"Of course! Cigar?" Churchill asked Eric.

"I am only eleven," replied the boy, "and my mum told me never to smoke. She always said it was a filthy habit."

"Oh yes! Quite! Quite! Best not, then."

Gertrude, meanwhile, had other ideas. She reached her big, hairy hand into the box and snatched a cigar.

"No, Gertrude!" exclaimed the boy, but it was too late. The gorilla was munching on the cigar like it was a bar of chocolate.

MUNCH! MUNCH! MUNCH!

However, her face soon soured as she realised this wasn't something tasty at all. Then she began spitting out the pieces of cigar one by one.

"SPUT! SPUT! SPUT!"

A chewed-up lump of cigar paper landed in Winston Churchill's eye.

SPLURT!

"I am terribly sorry, sir!" said Eric.

Taking it all in his stride, Churchill whipped the silk handkerchief from his breast pocket, and wiped his eye. "Oh! Please don't worry. I've had much more badly behaved guests here at **Ten Downing Street**! Believe me! Ha! Ha! Ha!"

This broke the ice a little, and they all had a chuckle, even Gertrude.

"HOO! HOO!"

This made the gorilla spray even more cigar over everybody.

"HA! HA! HA!"

"Now I have to tell you," began Churchill, "that this whole Nazi plot has to remain top secret. If the British people and our allies knew quite how close Mr Hitler got to having me and all the rest of us killed, it would lower morale, and hurt the war effort. Do you understand?"

Eric and Sid suddenly sat up very straight.

"Yes, sir!" replied Eric.

"Oh!" added Sid, clearly deflated. By the looks of it, he'd wanted the whole world to know all about his heroism.

"This story will remain in the British Intelligence vaults for eighty years, like many national secrets, and then, and only then, will the file finally be released."

"We understand," agreed Sid reluctantly.

Gertrude put her finger up to her lips in a mime that said, **"TOP SECRET!"**

"But we do need a code name for this operation of yours? Do you have any suggestions?" asked the PM.

"We already have one!" exclaimed the boy.

"Well, I'm not sure it's quite…" began Sid.

"Please! Let me hear it!" insisted Churchill.

"CODE NAME BANANAS!" said Eric proudly.

Churchill chuckled so much he nearly fell off his chair.

"HA! HA! HA!"

"Do you like it?" asked the boy.

"I love it!

CODE NAME BANANAS

it is!"

CHAPTER | **65**

TOP SECRET

"I feel rotten I can't make a great big song and dance of this for you all," continued Churchill. "There must be something! We must have a celebration of some sort! You all like tea parties, don't you?"

"YES!" exclaimed the boy.

"This afternoon at *Buckingham Palace*, then!" exclaimed Churchill. "I will telephone the King at once and tell him the whole story!"

"*Buckingham Palace!*" spluttered Sid.

"My goodness!" added the boy.

"HOO!" hooted Gertrude.

"The monkey can come too!" said Churchill.

Sid and Eric shared a look. Who was going to tell the prime minister that gorillas were not monkeys but apes? No one!

"Is there anyone you three would like to invite?" asked Churchill.

"Well, there is someone I can think of," said Eric, "who helped us in this adventure."

"Who?" pressed Sid.

"Bessie!"

A bashful grin spread across Sid's face. "Yes, of course, we have to invite Bessie."

"I will ask them to lay a place for this Bessie!"

"And, sir?" asked the boy.

"Yes, young man?"

"Is it all right if we invite some of Gertrude's animal friends too?"

Churchill smiled at the thought. "I will have to check with the King, but as far as I am concerned the more the merrier! We will celebrate with tea and cake, and probably the odd glass of brandy and a cigar or two this very afternoon! Until then, Merry Christmas!"

"It's **CHRISTMAS?**" asked the boy, who had completely lost track of the days.

"Very nearly. It's Christmas Eve today. I know it's just a tea party, but I want you to know you are heroes.

Mighty great heroes."

This brought a tear to Sid's eye. Stepping on that mine on his very first day as a soldier all those years ago in the First World War had made him feel like a failure. But here was the prime minister, Winston Churchill himself, calling him a **hero!**

"Thank you so much, sir," exclaimed the old man.

"And I am going to personally recommend you to the King for the **George Cross.**"

Eric and Gertrude hugged Sid to share his excitement, but the man was overcome.

"But... but... but..."

"No buts, my good man!" declared Churchill. "You, sir, deserve one of the highest honours in the land. As do all of you. I wish I could give you, Eric and Gertrude, medals too, but they are not awarded to children or indeed gorillas. Apologies."

"You don't know how much this means to me, sir!"

exclaimed a misty-eyed Sid.

"And we'll get you fitted for some new legs pronto! And if there is anything I can do for you, boy, anything at all, then name it!"

Eric pondered this for a moment. He didn't have a single toy or game or book to his name. But the boy didn't want anything for himself. He wanted something for someone else…

"Well, Mr Churchill, sir," began Eric, "because we took Gertrude from the zoo we are in deep doo-doo, erm, I mean, trouble."

"Go on!" prompted the prime minister.

"Well, my Uncle Sid here lost his job at **LONDON ZOO**, and… well…" spluttered Eric, looking at Sid. "Well, he's worked there all his life and is the best zookeeper in the whole wide world! I wondered, I just wondered, whether you might have a word with the zoo director, Sir Frederick Frown, and ask for Sidney Pratt to be given his job back!"

Tears shone in Sid's eyes.

"Consider it done! I will call him at once!"

"Oh, thank you!" exclaimed the boy. "And when you speak to him please can you make sure no one ever tries to harm my beautiful friend Gertrude here."

"I read in yesterday's newspapers there was a big hunt on for her. Yes, you have my word. I will tell Frown that no one is ever to harm this magnificent creature. Ever. Certainly not these three fools you told me all about: Frown, Batter and Gnarl!"

Eric and Sid smiled, and hugged Gertrude tightly. She gave them both smackers on their cheeks.

"MWAH! MWAH!"

"Now don't dilly-dally!" commanded Churchill. **"Put on your Sunday best. In just a few hours we will be taking tea with *royalty!*"**

CHAPTER | **66** |

PARTY AT THE PALACE

Later that afternoon, the dining room of *Buckingham Palace* was host to the greatest Christmas party ever held. King George VI, his wife, Queen Elizabeth, and their young daughters, Elizabeth and Margaret, were hosting not just the prime minister, Winston Churchill, but some wonderful new friends too.

Sitting around the impossibly long dining table in a room glistening with Christmas decorations were, of course, Eric and Sid. The old man was sporting his First World War army uniform. On his jacket, King George had just pinned the **George Cross,** the medal that is one of the highest honours in Britain. From the blue ribbon dangled a silver cross. The cross depicted St George and the dragon, and two words, **"FOR GALLANTRY"**. Sid was beaming with pride as Bessie fed him slices of Victoria sponge cake.

"My hero!" she sighed.

However, what made this royal tea party so special were the animals. There were creatures of all shapes and sizes, which delighted the young princesses no end. They giggled together with Eric as:

Parker the one-winged parrot pecked at a Christmas pudding.

SQUAWK!

Ernie the elephant had his stumpy trunk stuck in a blancmange.

WHOOMPH!

Sassy the blind seal munched on some salmon sandwiches.

MUNCH!

Totter the tortoise looked as if he were taking part in a competition to eat his yule log the slowest.

YUM!

Florence the one-legged flamingo nibbled at a Christmas cake.

PECK! PECK! PECK!

Colin the crocodile slurped up some nice soft jelly without his lack of teeth stopping him.

"SLURP!"

Botty the one-armed and big-bottomed baboon bounced up and down on her ginormous bottom, having just discovered the joys of mince pies.

BOING! BOING! BOING!

MUNCH! MUNCH! MUNCH!

However, the star of the show, as always, was Gertrude. The gorilla had a huge banana split all to herself. It was made of bananas, cherries, marshmallows, nuts and, of course, ice cream. She was making her way through it at an astonishing rate, spraying bits of banana all over the royal family as she ate.

CHOMP! CHOMP! CHOMP!

SPLURT! SPLURT! SPLURT!

"HOO!"

"Papa!" pleaded the eldest daughter, Elizabeth, who was fourteen. "Please can we have our very own gorilla for Christmas?"

"N-n-no, d-d-darling!" stammered the King, plucking pieces of banana out of his hair.

"Not fair!" snapped the ten-year-old Margaret, banging her spoon hard on the table.

CLANG!

"Watch your manners, dear!" reminded the Queen.

But with a palace full of animals, manners were not on display today.

Princess Elizabeth turned to Eric. "How do you do?" she asked stiffly.

"How do I do what?" he asked.

This made her smile. "I mean, how are you?"

"Oh sorry. I am well, thank you, Your Royal Highness!"

"Forgive me, but I can detect a sadness in your eyes."

"That's because I am an orphan."

"I am so sorry."

"It's all right. But I don't know where I'll be for Christmas…"

"Well, Eric, I am sure you can join us here at the palace, if you like?" replied the princess.

"That's very kind of you!" interrupted Sid. "But, well, Bessie and I have been talking and…"

But before Sid could say another word Bessie leaped in.

"We're engaged!" she hooted.

CHAPTER 67

BANANA SPLIT

"WOWZERS!" exclaimed the boy.

"Yes! Rather!" agreed the princess. "Wowzers it is!"

"You helped me realise, Eric," began Sid, "that the love of my life was right next door! My Bessie!"

"My Sidney!" cooed Bessie as she pulled the old man's face to hers and gave him a big, slobbery kiss.

"MWAH!"

"All right! All right! Save it for the wedding!" said Sid. "So, Eric, I want you to come and live with me and Bessie!"

"Really?" asked the boy, his eyes widening with delight.

"Yes, our Eric!" hollered Bessie. "We want to adopt you and all the animals, so we can all be one big, happy family."

The boy's eyes welled with tears. "I don't know why

I'm crying!" he said. "They are happy tears, I promise!"

Without a word, Sid and Bessie gave the boy a cuddle at the same time. Eric was in the middle, just as he had been with his mum and dad. It wasn't so much a cuddle as a **MUDDLE**.

Even Gertrude joined in too!

"HOOO!"

"Well, it looks as if this story has a happy ending, after all," said Princess Elizabeth. "More tea?"

"I think Gertrude would love another banana split, please!" replied Eric. "She is bananas about bananas!"

The gorilla nodded and rubbed her tummy eagerly.

"I will inform the cook!" said the princess.

In no time, the biggest banana split the world had ever seen was carried into the dining room by an army of footmen and put down in the middle of the table for all the animals to enjoy.

This would prove to be a BIG MISTAKE!

Now, I don't know if you've ever seen a large group of animals share a GIANT BANANA SPLIT all at once, but things can very quickly get out of hand. Soon the tea party descended into CHAOS!

It is impossible to say exactly who threw what, but in no time the palace dining room was host to the most humongous FOOD FIGHT!

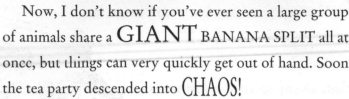

SPLOT!

SPLUT! SPLASH!

Sid and Bessie were first to be hit by a huge dollop of ice cream.

"Oh my!" hooted Bessie.

Next a chocolate-covered banana landed right in the King's face.

SPLAT!

"I am so sorry, Your Majesty!" said Sid.

"D-d-don't worry, my g-g-good man!" stammered the King. "I haven't had so much f-f-fun in years!"

With that, he picked up a big bowl of trifle and emptied it over his wife's head.

WHOOMPH!

The two princesses burst into fits of laughter.

"HA! HA! HA!"

The Queen wasn't having any of that, so she splatted a jam tart in each of their faces.

"Take that!" she cried, giggling at how absurd this all was. "TEE-HEE!"

Having faces full of jam just made the girls laugh even more.

"HA! HA! HA!"

The prime minister was beginning to feel left out.

"Come on!" implored Churchill. "Give me your best shot!"

He closed his eyes, and a yule log was promptly stuck in the old man's face by the mischievous Margaret.

SPLURGE!

"Delicious!" was the prime minister's verdict as he licked the chocolate icing from around his mouth. Then, smirking with delight, he picked up the blancmange and hurled it across the table.

WHOOSH!

SPLAT!

It splattered all over Eric and Gertrude, who licked up every last bit with glee.

"SLURP! SLURP!"

In no time, everyone in the room was laughing. For a couple of hours that **CHRISTMAS EVE OF 1940,** the war and the world of suffering it had created was briefly forgotten in a great big celebration. A celebration of what it is to be alive.

Life.

Love.

Laughter.

Churchill stood up, filled his glass with brandy and proposed a toast. The prime minister had just cheated death, so it seemed only fitting that he proposed, "To life!"

"TO LIFE!"

EPILOGUE

If you visit **LONDON ZOO** one day, you might just spot a very old zookeeper.

He is the one you will find in the middle of the biggest **muddle** with all the animals.

His name badge reads: **"ERIC GROUT"**.

In his trouser pocket, he always carries his Great-uncle Sid's George Cross.

It reminds him of the extraordinary adventures he shared with him, Bessie and, of course, his best friend in the world, Gertrude.

They may be long gone, but the three will be in his heart forever.

When a baby gorilla was born at the zoo, Eric was asked to name her.

He chose the name **"Gertrude".**

THE END

This story has remained top secret until now. The file, which has just been released, is called

It is the book you have just finished reading.

NOTES ON THE REAL WARTIME BRITAIN

Code Name Bananas is a story imagined by David Walliams, so some of the extraordinary things you have just enjoyed reading might never have actually happened in real life. But as the author has set this story in 1940 you might be interested in learning more about wartime Britain, as well as some of the real inspirations behind this book.

The Second World War started in 1939 when Germany invaded Poland, which Britain and France had promised to protect. It ended in September 1945. It was fought between the Axis powers (including Germany, Italy and Japan) and the Allies (including Britain, France, the USA, Canada, Australia, New Zealand, India, China and, from 1941 onwards, the Soviet Union). The war changed the lives of everyone in Britain, with food and other goods in short supply. German U-boats patrolled the Atlantic, attacking cargo ships, so valuable supplies were lost. In addition, people left jobs in farming and food production to fight in the war. Some food was rationed to make sure there was enough to go around, and people were encouraged to grow fruit and vegetables in their gardens. Bananas would have been a rare treat.

Adolf Hitler was the leader of the Nazi party and seized power as Chancellor of Germany. He believed in the absolute supremacy of the German people, and during the war he ordered millions of Jews, Romani and other groups to be murdered in the

Holocaust. He undertook a military campaign to occupy much of Europe and planned to invade Britain. Hitler took the title "Führer", demanding complete loyalty from the German people and enforcing his total control as dictator.

The Blitz was a German bombing campaign in 1940 and 1941 that targeted big cities like London, Manchester and Coventry, destroying thousands of homes, and forcing people to take cover in bomb shelters and even London Underground stations. More than two million children were evacuated to the countryside so they'd be safe from the German air raids. However, while this story has anti-aircraft guns in the centre of London for added drama, they were actually located on the outskirts. Bombs did indeed fall on London Zoo, as happens in the story. At one time, this resulted in a zebra escaping on to the streets of London!

The Dunkirk evacuation was the rescue of over 300,000 Allied soldiers from the port of Dunkirk, in northern France, in May and June 1940. Belgian, French and British forces were trapped in the area by the German army, and massively outnumbered. In a huge military operation, most of these soldiers were rescued by ships from the Royal Navy and French Navy, as well as a large number of ordinary people in private boats. Just like in the story, several Allied ships were unfortunately sunk by German boats and planes. In real life, the *Grafton*, Eric's father's ship, *was* torpedoed by a U-boat, killing several men on board, although, in fact, that did not cause it to sink, and many of the men were able to be saved.

German U-boats played a significant role in the Second World War, threatening Allied cargo ships, as well as attacking the Royal Navy. In fact, breaking the code that these submarines used to communicate was one of the things that helped the Allies win the war. As far as we know, though, a U-boat never sailed up the Thames.

London Zoo remained open during most of the war, but at the time of this story it is probable that the elephants and some of the other animals had been evacuated to Whipsnade Zoo to keep them safe. Sadly, just like in the story, some of the more dangerous and venomous creatures did have to be put down in case the zoo was damaged by bombing and they escaped. London Zoo has always cared for its animals' welfare as well as its visitors, and, in fact, during the Second World War, wounded soldiers were allowed into the zoo for free.

Many incredible things happen to the animal characters in this story. We know that in real life wild animals should be left in their natural habitats as far as is possible. Today, zoos around the world, including London Zoo, focus on the conservation of endangered species and on creating suitable environments for the animals for which they care.

Winston Churchill was prime minister during the war, and his military leadership played a big part in the eventual Allied victory. After leaving school with poor exam results, he became a soldier and part-time journalist before going into politics. The stirring speeches he gave to the British people are famous for having kept up the morale of the nation.

Buckingham Palace: Eric and Sid enjoy a party at the palace with the young princesses Elizabeth and Margaret. It is fun to imagine them sharing a banana split with Gertrude. The young Princess Elizabeth went on to become our queen, and as Queen Elizabeth II she sits on the throne today.